Grandpa—and Me

OTHER YEARLING BOOKS YOU WILL ENJOY:

Mildred Murphy, How Does Your Garden Grow?,
PHYLLIS GREEN

Wild Violets, PHYLLIS GREEN

Kitty in the Summer, JUDY DELTON

Beat the Turtle Drum, CONSTANCE C. GREENE

Ramona and Her Mother, BEVERLY CLEARY

Ramona and Her Father, BEVERLY CLEARY

Secret Lives, BERTHE AMOSS

Don't Ask Miranda, LILA PERL

Dumb Like Me, Olivia Potts, LILA PERL

What If They Knew?, PATRICIA HERMES

YEARLING BOOKS are designed especially to entertain and enlighten young people. Charles F. Reasoner, Professor of Elementary Education, New York University, is consultant to this series.

For a complete listing of all Yearling titles, write to Education Sales Department, Dell Publishing Co., Inc., 1 Dag Hammarskjold Plaza, New York, New York 10017.

Grandpa—and Me

Stephanie S. Tolan

A YEARLING BOOK

Published by
Dell Publishing Co., Inc.
1 Dag Hammarskjold Plaza
New York, New York 10017

ISBN: 0-440-43260-X

Reprinted by arrangement with Charles Scribner's Sons
Printed in the United States of America
First Yearling printing—April 1982

CW

For my grandfathers,
ALBERT SCHROY *and* JOSEPH STEIN.
Time chose for one,
One chose for himself.

Grandpa—and Me

MONDAY, JULY 14, 9:30 a.m.

My grandfather is crazy. I know that's a rotten thing to say, and I've been telling myself all morning that only a really crummy person would say it. But I believe in being honest and—well—there isn't anything else to call it. He's stark, staring crazy! Even though he has lived with us practically all my life, I only found out about it this morning. Or else he went crazy for the first time during the night last night.

Let me tell you something about him first, before I have to think about how I know he's crazy. My grandfather is eighty years old, but he doesn't usually seem that old to me. He has this pure white hair and a neat little white mustache and he seems taller than he really is because he always stands and walks very straight. He keeps his body in very good condition and walks a lot. When he was younger he was an athlete—not a pro or anything, but good at practically all sports. "Kerry," he'd say to me, "keep your body in good condition and it'll pay you back. Don't sit when you can stand, don't walk when you can run." He taught me to swim when I wasn't even in school yet, and swimming is still just about my favorite thing in the world. I'm going to be a butterfly champion someday, and I swim at the pool in the park every single day all summer.

Grandpa's been living with us since I was about three, just after Grandma died. My brother Matt, who is almost fourteen and getting a little strange himself, says he can remember Grandma a little, but the closest I can come is sometimes when I go into somebody's house there's a cooking smell or just a house smell that makes me think of the house my grandparents used to live in. But Matt's two years older than I am so he naturally remembers more. I can't imagine what it would be like not to have Grandpa living with us.

His favorite things have always been sports and rocks. He's a real rock hound and hardly goes anywhere without keeping his eyes on the ground in case some really unusual rock should pop up suddenly. When Matt and I were little he used to take us rock hunting a lot. We were mostly interested in exploring the woods or the hills and eating the picnic lunch we always had along, so neither of us learned much about rocks. But we had lots of fun with him. "Rock hunting keeps them out in the fresh air," he used to tell Mom. "It keeps them moving." Since Mom was usually working anyway, I guess she was just glad to have us go with Grandpa.

Now, suddenly, here I am saying he's crazy. And trying to avoid thinking about how I know. When I woke up this morning, the first thing I thought about was the weather. I just decided yesterday that I'm going to become a butterfly champion. I was at the pool practicing the butterfly stroke and Kevin, the really neat lifeguard, was saying that the butterfly is just about the hardest stroke and that nobody he knows much likes doing it. So I decided to be a champion. I figured I wouldn't have all that much competition, and in two years, if I work really hard, I might get good enough for the Olympics or something. So, today was to be the first day of my new program to become a champ, and I was hot to get to the pool the minute it opened and start working. I jumped right out of bed and pulled my shade up to see what it was like outside. I could tell it was going to be a good day.

Then I saw Grandpa. He had just come out the back door, and I could hardly believe what I was seeing. He had his pants on inside-out—with the white pockets flapping around on the outside. And on his head he had his old rock hunting hat with the torn brim that Mom had convinced him to stop wearing because it was so ratty looking. We thought he'd given it to Goodwill.

Now the way he was dressed was crazy enough, but that wasn't all. He walked to the middle of the backyard and sort of reached out into the air and took hold of some kind of handle that wasn't there. He opened this imaginary door, went through it, and closed it behind him. Then he started fussing around with his pants. For a second I thought maybe he'd looked down and noticed that he had them on inside-out—but that wasn't it. He was trying to work the zipper, which was naturally on the inside. And then he did what I keep wishing I hadn't seen and didn't have to remember. He peed. Right there in the middle of our backyard in front of God and everybody. Well, not everybody, because it was pretty early and nobody but me was even up, much less looking out in the backyard. But anybody might have been up. And anybody might have seen him!

As soon as I saw what he was doing, I pulled my shade back down—like if I couldn't see it, maybe it wasn't really happening. I waited a minute or two and then put the shade up again. He'd finished by then and was just going out the back gate toward the park. At first I was glad he was going, but then I remembered how he was dressed and I began to think about all the people who'd see him. And then I thought about what would happen if he did what he'd just done in the backyard while he was in the park. Of course they have rest rooms in the park, but he's got his very own bathroom downstairs, just across the hall from his room, and that didn't keep him from going in the yard.

I sat there by my window for a long time, trying to decide what to do. The idea of him in the park looking like that made me feel terrible, but the thought of going to the park to get him and walking all the way home with him seemed even worse. Just then Mom and Dad got up and started getting ready to go to work, and I thought about telling them, but I just couldn't get myself to do it. Maybe it was me who was crazy—maybe I had just imagined the whole thing. Maybe it was a dream and I'd never even gotten out of bed yet. But I knew better, because if I do dream I don't remember it very often, and this was very, very real.

So I chickened out and didn't do anything at

all, just sat there wishing I hadn't seen him. Dad went off to work, and then Mom called upstairs to tell me she was leaving. She was in a crummy mood, I knew, because she had to show a house clear on the other side of town to some people she didn't think really intended to buy a house anyway, and she hated to waste the time. She told me to be sure I had a decent breakfast, and then she went too, and it was too late to tell anyone. Matt wasn't up yet—he's hardly ever moving around before noon, and then he only gets a peanut butter toast and goes down to the basement room he's fixed up with a stereo set, and listens to music. He hardly even acts like a member of the family anymore—just goes his own way and has his buddies over and stays locked in that room down there blasting his music all through the house so the bass vibrates my whole room. I couldn't tell Matt.

There was one person I could tell, and I wanted more than anything to tell her and ask her advice. My friend Jeannie is not just my best friend, she's the smartest person I know, and if anyone could tell me what to do about Grandpa, it'd be Jeannie. But she's way out west at Yellowstone Park on vacation with her family and won't be back for two more weeks. I can't even call her up! So I'm left with talking to you, tape recorder, which is practically the same as talking to myself, since you can't talk back.

Sometimes I hate summer vacation, when everybody goes away. We never go anywhere, because Mom doesn't want to go away during the summer. She says it's too good a time for selling houses to go away then. And in the winter, when the real estate business isn't so great, Matt and I have school. So we just never do get a decent vacation, and I have to stay home all summer while everybody else goes off camping or to a resort somewhere and all I can do is go to the park and swim. That's why I'm going to be a butterfly champion. At least working for that gives me something to do!

But once I thought about that again, I remembered Grandpa at the park, dressed crazy. And I thought about Kevin, the lifeguard, seeing him like that. Everybody knows he's my grandfather. I'd be so embarrassed I'd die. And pretty soon there will be lots more people in the park—lots of kids from school. And what if he peed right out in the open? I could just imagine the police bringing him home or worse—taking him to the police station and calling Mom or Dad. After all, he isn't some four-year-old whose mother lets him use the bushes when the john is too far away! So I know I'll have to go to the park and get him and bring him home. At times like this I wish I were more like Jeannie. She doesn't ever seem to care what other people think. She just does what she wants to do or what she has to do and pays no attention to anybody. If only it were raining, I could take an umbrella and keep it over my face.

MONDAY, JULY 14, 11:30 a.m.

I found Grandpa in the park and managed to get him home. But it was just about the worst experience of my whole life. He was sitting on his favorite bench when I got there, just where he always sits to wait for the man he plays chess and shuffleboard with. The only thing different was the way he was dressed. There were some little kids playing in the sandbox near the bench, and they were pointing and laughing, but he just laughed back at them, like they had some kind of special joke between them. He didn't seem to understand that they were making fun of him.

When he saw me he waved and grinned and acted like he'd been expecting me. That was a little crazy too, because we haven't gone to the park together—or done much of anything together, now that I think about it—for a long time. He wanted me to go for a walk with him—rock hunting, I guess. But I told him that I'd come to get him to take him back for the special breakfast I'd made. I hadn't planned to say that, I hadn't planned anything about how I'd get him home, and there wasn't time to work it out very well. I figured I'd be able to come up with some kind of breakfast besides dry cereal, if I could only get him home. I can't cook a single thing except grilled cheese sandwiches, but I figured the pancake mix box would have to have directions on it. Anyway, the important thing was to get him away from those bratty little kids who were starting to call him names.

"Breakfast? You fixed a special breakfast for me?" he said, and when I saw how happy it made him, I could have kicked myself for lying. It had been so long since I had done anything with Grandpa, or even thought about him much, that he must have felt really good that I'd bothered. He stood up, still not noticing the way he was dressed, and ran his hand through my hair the way he used to all the time when I was little. "Let's jog! We need a good appetite for his special occasion."

I pictured myself jogging alongside this old man with the inside-out pants, and wished for an umbrella again. But I knew he could jog, and that he wouldn't want to walk—as if he had to keep me from getting lazy. So I did my best to look as if I liked the idea, and off we want. The only thing I did was take a little detour around the south end of the park so we wouldn't have to pass the swimming pool, which would be opening right about then. Even with the longer route, Grandpa kept up with me easily, and when we got home, he was hardly even breathing fast. Whatever had happened to his mind during the night hadn't affected his body at all.

We didn't pass many people on the way home, and when we did, I tried to pretend I was a guard from a mental institution, capturing an escaped patient. I guess it probably didn't matter anyway, though. It's unusual enough to see an old man and a kid jogging—people must have thought we were playing some kind of game. Nobody paid much attention to us.

My pancakes didn't turn out to be very good. The first ones didn't cook quite through. I guess the pan wasn't hot enough. And the next ones got burned on one side. But Grandpa didn't seem to notice. He ate them anyway and told me all about the shuffleboard game he won yesterday with Mr. Buhler, his park friend. "Shuffleboard isn't much of a sport," he said when he had finished and was wiping his mustache with his napkin. "But poor old Max Buhler has let himself get so run-down that it's the most active thing he can manage. I almost always win. Luckily for him, he's a chess player, or he'd never know what winning means!" He got up from the table and glanced down at his pants as he was pushing in his chair. For just a minute, I thought he was going to say something. He got a funny frown on his face when he saw his pockets flapping out like that. But he just rubbed his head a little and thanked me for the breakfast. "I—I think I'll go to my room and rest a little," he said. "That was a long jog you took me on, you know."

Just as he was leaving the kitchen, Matt scruffed in wearing an old, dirty pair of cut-offs, looking like he'd just dragged himself out of bed. When he saw Grandpa he opened his mouth to say something, but I gave him a look even Matt couldn't miss, so he shut his mouth again.

"What a mess this kitchen is," he said after Grandpa's door had closed. "You cooking, huh? What was it, wallpaper paste? And what's with Grandpa in those pants . . .?"

At that, I started to cry and rushed up to my room and slammed the door. Matt didn't follow me. Not that I expected him to—he's too locked inside his own little world to worry about anybody else. Even if he had wanted to know what was wrong, I'm not sure I could have told him exactly. All I know is that this has so far been the most horrible day of my life, and Grandpa's crazy, and one minute I want to find some way to lock him in his room or something so he can't go back outside like that, and the next minute I remember all the things we've done together, and mostly I want to cry.

MONDAY, JULY 14, 4:00 p.m.

Mom came home for lunch around one, griping about the people who weren't going to buy that house, and exploded when she saw the mess I'd made in the kitchen. But when I told her I'd made pancakes for Grandpa, she settled right down. Grandpa was still in his room, so I decided not to say anything to her yet. She fixed us each a tuna sandwich and helped me clean up the kitchen before she went back to the office. Matt was in his basement room with his stereo on as usual. She called down a good-bye before she left, but the music didn't stop, and I doubt if Matt even heard her. A little while later David

Melkerson came over and went downstairs. The music went right on. I thought about going to the pool, and then I thought about jogging home with Grandpa this morning and decided I could begin my butterfly championship program tomorrow.

Since Jeannie wasn't around to talk to, I decided to try to imagine I was Jeannie and work on my problem systematically, the way she would. So I went up to my room and sat at my desk with some paper in front of me and began to think. Jeannie always says that the first thing you have to do when you have a problem to work out is to be as honest with yourself about how you feel as you can. Then you write down whatever you feel on a piece of paper. She says you have to write it down to keep your mind from wandering. Then you write down all the other things you know about the problem, and then you take everything you've written and read it over and think about it. Eventually, she says, you can always figure out what to do if you're complete enough and honest enough!

I headed my first page "Grandpa" and then sat there looking at it for a while. I didn't know what to put next. Grandpa is a member of the family, that's all. What could I put down? So I decided to write down what I knew about his coming to live with us. When I was three, my grandma had a stroke and died. It was very sudden and unexpected. Mom says it's ironic that Grandma died first, because there are lots more widows in the world than widowers and nobody ever expected Grandpa to be left alone like that. I've always thought that if Grandpa had been the one who had died, Grandma would have gone right on living in their house pretty much the same way, taking care of herself. But Grandpa didn't know the first thing about keeping a house or cooking or anything. So he moved in with us practically the minute she died. It's funny—Mom has tried so hard to be sure Matt knows all about taking care of himself so that could never happen to him that he's the one who knows how to cook and I'm the one who can't make anything but cold cereal and grilled cheese sandwiches. Maybe Mom thinks girls learn that stuff automatically.

Anyway, Grandpa has always been around. There isn't a single other kid in my class who has a grandparent living with them. Of course some of them have really young grandparents. In fact, Jeannie's grandparents aren't all that much older than my parents. Mom didn't have Matt for a long time after she married Dad because she was so busy selling houses and making money that she didn't think she'd even bother having kids at all. Matt was an accident. We all know it, but it doesn't bother him because Mom has always told everyone what a great accident it was and how, if Matt hadn't come along, she'd never have known how wonderful it could be to have a family. I guess she liked having one kid pretty well because she had me on purpose when Matt was only two. When I was little, Mom worked pretty much, and sometimes I got the feeling I knew Grandpa better than I knew Mom, because he was more likely to be home with us than she was. He wasn't a babysitter exactly, but after school we could always count on him being there, and we'd talk about what we'd done that day over the milk and cookies he'd always have ready. Or he'd take us for walks or help us with the rock collections he was always trying to get us interested in.

Lately, though—the last couple of years, I guess—it's been harder and harder to have Grandpa around. Matt and I don't need somebody to be home with us so much any more, and neither of us is interested in rocks, no matter how hard Grandpa's tried. He doesn't understand much about what we've been doing in school, and we're mostly pretty busy in the afternoons anyway—Matt with baseball or basketball practice or his stereo, and me with swimming or doing stuff with Jeannie. Sometimes he seems old now because he doesn't really understand what we like to do or what we're interested in.

Grandpa is really the only old person I know. Mary Jane Hartnett has an old grandmother, but she's in a nursing home and Mary Jane just visits her sometimes. She isn't much like a member of the family. Mary Jane gets out of going whenever she can because she says the nursing home is ugly and smells terrible and is full of old people with no teeth who sit around in wheelchairs and make weird noises. Mom says that no human being should be sent to a place like that, and certainly not a person with a family. Maybe Mary Jane would agree. But maybe she wouldn't, too, because she doesn't have to think about her grandmother at all except those times when she can't get out of going to the nursing home.

There isn't too much talk about nursing homes in our family, but every once in a while Dad mentions it, and then we're in for a gigantic argument. Mom says that it's a daughter's duty to take care of her father when he can't take care of himself. Then Dad says, "So Joan is a daughter too, you know. And Dan is a son. Why can't your father stay with them sometimes, in the interest of keeping the family together and avoiding a nursing home?" I've always thought that was a pretty good argument, and maybe Mom does too, because whenever he says that, she says that if it were *his* father, he wouldn't be so anxious to get him out of the house. Then Dad says he isn't anxious to get Grandpa out of the house, and that he loves him, but that there are still times when he'd like to have just his own family to take care of.

It's silly for Mom to talk about what it would be like if it were Dad's father because both of his parents died before I was born. He always says they died the way he wants to—suddenly, and just about together. They both got sick, with flu or something, and died only a few hours apart, just a few days after they first got sick. There was never any worry about nursing homes in Dad's family.

I've never quite decided who I side with about nursing homes. Whenever there's something about one on TV, it's always bad—one that burned down and all the old people died, or one that's being closed down by the state for being dirty and unsafe. When those things come on TV, Mom always gives Dad these very significant looks. She doesn't think Grandpa notices, but I think he does, and I think he probably knows about the arguments, even though everybody's careful not to say anything when he's around. Grandpa's old, but he doesn't miss much. He's pretty sharp for a person his age—or at least he was before today—and I'm sure he doesn't want to go to any nursing home.

I'll bet it's terrible to know that the people you live with—your own family—even think about sending you someplace else! I've thought about how I'd feel if they started talking about sending me off to live with my aunts and uncles. Or to boarding school. A kid in our class got sent away to military school last year because his parents were getting a divorce and nobody much wanted to take care of him. I thought then that military school was kind of a nursing home for kids—a place people could send you when they didn't feel like having you around anymore. I guess, all in all, I'd have to agree with Mom. No matter how hard it can be sometimes, it's better to have Grandpa at home than to send him away.

Anyway, Mom always wins the arguments because Grandpa is her father and there really isn't anything anybody else can say. She works hard and earns enough money so that Dad can't even say he has to support Grandpa. The only time anything new was ever added to the whole argument was a few months ago after one of those TV specials when they went over the same old ground till Dad said he hoped Mom would see reason if Grandpa ever got sick, because it was obvious that we couldn't take care of him at home then. It was the first time I'd ever thought about the word "nursing" in nursing home—like they were hospitals or something—only friendlier. Until then I'd been thinking of them as old folks' homes. But when I thought about an old person who was sick, who needed real doctors and nurses, it didn't seem so bad.

Naturally, Mom pointed out that Grandpa was in better physical shape than practically anyone in the family, and had never had so much as a cold. So the subject was dropped again. But it made me think about nursing homes in a different way than ever before.

When I'd thought about all that, and even written some of it down, it didn't seem to help me figure out what to do. So I headed another sheet "Possible Craziness" and sat there looking at it. It just seemed impossible to think of Grandpa and craziness. He has always been so sensible—too sensible half the time. What could make somebody act crazy? I remembered how happy he'd been to see me in the park and how normal he'd seemed then, except for the pants. And then I remembered the strange look he got on his face when he'd finished the pancakes and noticed his pants. It was as if he were seeing them inside-out for the first time.

Then I had an idea that made the whole day seem better. Maybe he'd been sleepwalking! It had been awfully early when I first looked out the window. Maybe he had gotten up and dressed himself in his sleep! I crumpled up the second sheet of paper and threw it in the wastebasket. Sleepwalking! One time I heard Mom telling a friend that when Matt was little he got up in the night to go to the bathroom, but instead of turning left, he turned right, opened the door of the linen closet, and peed all over the clean sheets and towels. They had laughed and laughed, and I'd had to put my hand over my mouth and run to my room so they wouldn't know I'd been listening. I guess if Matt could do it, Grandpa could.

Jeannie is right. If you sit down and think about something hard enough, you can figure it out! It's a little scary to think that people can do stuff like that when they're sleeping, though. What if I woke up in the middle of the night and found myself standing in the garden outside Kevin's house in my pajamas? I hardly even have the nerve to talk to him about swimming at the pool, but I think about him a lot, and I'd just die if I did anything crazy in my sleep that would let anyone else know how I feel about him. I haven't even told Jeannie.

Thinking about Kevin reminded me that I haven't been to the pool all day. I'd better begin working on my butterfly stroke today after all!

SUNDAY, JULY 27, 5:00 p.m.

It's been two weeks, and Grandpa has been his old self the whole time, so I guess I was right—he was sleepwalking. I've been spending a lot of time at the pool, doing the butterfly. I finally told Kevin that I want to be a butterfly champion, and he offered to help. I'm getting pretty good, even if I do say so myself.

Jeannie's coming home tonight and will probably come over first thing in the morning with her journal. She keeps this journal which is something like a diary and something like what I do with you, tape recorder—telling about what I've been doing and what I'm thinking—but her journal is more than that. She puts all her most important thoughts and feelings in her journal in a really poetic way. She says when she does that she gets to know herself better than if she just thought about things and then forgot them. The work of writing them down exactly right helps her understand her feelings better. And she says that understanding her own thoughts and feelings helps her understand other people better, too. It's a little hard to follow Jeannie's theories sometimes, but there's no question that she's the smartest person I've ever known, and her journal must have something to do with it.

Anyway, I like to have her read it to me—when she wants to—because sometimes she writes about things we've done together and there are times when I really figure out how I felt about something when I listen to how she felt about it. Otherwise, I guess I'd miss a lot. She says she's training herself to be so observant that she never misses anything, so that when she gets older she can be either a scientist or a philosopher—she hasn't decided which. Hearing what she wrote on vacation is even better than getting letters while she's gone (she doesn't write much because she doesn't have time) and it's almost as good as being on the vacation myself.

We'll go to the pool first thing after she's read me her journal because I want her to time me swimming fifty meters. I can't keep a journal myself—English isn't one of my favorite subjects. I figure I get almost as much out of just telling my thoughts like this, without having to go to all the work of getting them written down right. But Jeannie doesn't even know about these tapes, and sometimes I get the feeling that in our relationship it is Jeannie who does everything really worth doing. So I want her to see how fast I'm getting at the butterfly. If she ever wins the Nobel Prize for literature or science or something, I want to have at least a swimming medal to hold up against it. Maybe it won't make us even, but I'll feel better anyway.

Ever since the morning Grandpa walked in his sleep I've been trying to be more observant about the family. And I haven't been too happy about what I've been seeing. I want to talk to Jeannie about it and see what she thinks, and I've been trying to get things as clear in my head as I can first.

The thing I've noticed most of all is that our family is a lot different than it used to be. When Matt and I were little, Grandpa took us places and talked with us and did things for us—like making Matt kites and teaching me to swim. I've thought about that a whole lot. The summer I was five Grandpa decided I had had enough time in the kiddie pool. So every day he took me to the big pool where he was practically the only man and for sure the oldest. And right in the middle of all those kids running around and splashing, with all those mothers sitting on their towels and watching, he taught me to swim. First he taught me to hold my breath and go underwater. He'd hold me in his arms and we'd jump up and down in the shallow water three times and go under—together. I can remember how it felt when we'd come up, me spluttering and choking and him with the water running off his hair and his mustache and both of us laughing like crazy. He'd make faces at me and wave underwater so I would open my eyes. Then he taught me to float and kick my feet. If there was ever anything I was afraid to do, he'd do it to show me how. By the time I was ready to go into the first grade that fall, I could swim and dive and go across the width of the pool underwater. And I was the only one in the first grade who could.

He taught Matt about baseball. They'd play catch for hours, and then he would pitch and pitch and pitch while Matt tried to hit home runs. When he did hit the ball Grandpa would run after it, always telling everybody how much he liked the exercise. He's the one who bought Matt his good glove and bat. And he took him to all the games he could find—like company teams playing other companies. Once he took both Matt and me to a major league game and said he'd had more fun than both of us put together. All I remember is the train ride into the city.

And always he kept telling us to keep in shape, to use our bodies and keep them strong. And always he kept busy with us, getting as much exercise and fun out of things as we did.

His own rock collection got bigger all the time, while ours both stayed small—but we never passed up a chance to rock-hunt with him because it was such fun to go, even when we came back empty-handed. He would always point out the plants we saw and the animals and the bugs and butterflies and snakes. Mom never wanted us to have a pet, but Grandpa helped us catch any living thing we saw, and we always managed to keep it for a day or two in the garage before we let it go.

Mom and Dad made a special effort to do things with us after work and on weekends. The more I think back, the more I remember doing with Grandpa.

But all that was when I was little. I guess the first to change was Matt. He joined Little League, even though Grandpa said that it was too organized and too competitive to build good sports and good athletes. Matt wouldn't listen. He wanted to play with other kids, and Little League seemed like the best way. Grandpa went with him for a while, but he used to complain about how the coach pushed everybody too hard to win games. Matt would tell him if he didn't like the way things were run, he shouldn't go, and finally he did quit going. We still went rock hunting some, but Matt began to be busy all the time and didn't have much time for that.

Then I joined the Y so I could swim in the winter as well as in the summer and I started going after school twice a week. They didn't let people watch the classes, so Grandpa couldn't come with me after the first couple of lessons. I hate to think about it now, but it's true that I had gotten sort of embarrassed that my grandfather was teaching me and swimming with me, so I was glad to be in a regular class just like other kids, even though they were mostly older because I could swim so well for my age.

It must have been about then that Grandpa met Max Buhler in the park and began playing chess and shuffleboard. He walks a lot and jogs some, but Mr. Buhler doesn't like all that activity, so Grandpa has to go alone. I figure he hasn't added much to his rock collection in a long time either, since nobody goes rock hunting with him anymore.

When I really think about it, I don't know what Grandpa has been doing with himself lately. Mom and Dad don't seem to save time to do things with him much anymore. We see him at dinner and we know he goes to the park a lot. Mom gave him a television for his room two

Christmases ago and I guess he watches that a lot. And sometimes I play cards with him in the evening if I don't have homework.

Maybe the sleepwalking had something to do with how things have changed around here. Maybe he has so little to do when he's awake that his mind gives him dreams of doing things when he's asleep and maybe that one morning he really did them. And if he does know about Mom and Dad and their nursing home arguments, that could sure give him nightmares.

Anyway, the more I've thought about him the rottener I've felt. None of us has been treating him very well lately. And even though Mom says she wants to keep him here with the family, she doesn't do anything to make us feel more like a family. Or anything to make him feel like he belongs. And when I am as honest with myself as I can be, I have to admit that I don't want to do stuff like rock hunting with Grandpa anymore. I'm just too selfish!

Meanwhile, Matt is getting worse and worse to everybody. He hasn't said more than ten words to anyone in the last week. The other night at dinner Mom told him she wanted him to stop playing his stereo in the early afternoon so that Grandpa could take a nap during the hottest part of the day. Matt said it was his house too and he ought to be able to play his own stereo in his own room without a lot of hassle. He stomped away from the table and didn't come back for dessert.

I watched Grandpa's face really close all that time, because I figured it would make him feel kind of bad and might even be enough to make him sleepwalk again, but he was so busy cutting the corn off his corncob that I couldn't be sure he even heard what Matt had said. Anyway, it isn't as though Matt was being nasty just to Grandpa—he's been behaving like an all-round creep all the time. Mom and Dad exchanged some more of their meaningful glances and then we started talking about something else. The next day Matt bought a pair of earphones and the whole house has been quieter ever since, so it turned out fine.

Today I asked Grandpa to go for a walk with me. I figured I could do at least that much a couple of times a week. And we actually had a great time. He took me along the creek to a place where he'd found a fossil rock with a whole, perfect trilobite fossil. He'd covered it up and left it there instead of taking it home with him because he wanted to show one of us where he'd found it, so I really felt good about suggesting the walk. And I'd never seen a whole trilobite except in the museum anyway. I'm going to show it to Jeannie sometime when I feel like impressing her!

On the way home we went past the pool, and

the sign-up sheet for the end-of-the-summer municipal meet was on the bulletin board. Grandpa wanted me to try everything, but I signed up for the butterfly, a relay, and an underwater distance race. He offered to coach me in the mornings and I almost said no, but caught myself in time. Kevin teaches beginners' classes in the morning and hasn't got time for me then anyway. So I'll have some time with Grandpa almost every day.

I guess it just doesn't pay to panic. Things are okay after all.

MONDAY, JULY 28, 1:00 p.m.

I am going into hibernation. I will not see anybody, not even Jeannie, ever again. She is no longer my best friend. I have no friends. I will not be in the swimming meet, I will not see Kevin again, I will not set foot into any water ever. Not ever. By the time I am thirty years old nobody except Matt and my parents will even remember that I ever existed.

It happened this morning, and Mom and Dad are very worried. They'd be a lot more worried if they knew what I know. I'm not just worried, because I know the truth. He wasn't sleepwalking that day after all. Grandpa really is crazy! I've heard that crazy people can pretend to be as sane as anybody and even fool the doctors. Well, that must be what Grandpa has been doing for the last two weeks. And all the time I've been trying to think of ways to make things the way they used to be! No more. Nothing can be the same when someone has gone crazy! And now they won't take him to a nursing home anyway. They'll take him to an asylum and lock him up.

When it started I was the only one in the family here again. Jeannie came over first thing this morning with her journal. We came up to my room and closed the door so we wouldn't be disturbed, even though Matt was already off playing ball, and she started reading me her journal. It was really terrific—full of deep thoughts like geysers meaning eternal life and the devil's boiling pot really looking as if somewhere underground there is something evil that can't be kept down forever. There were some other things I really liked, but I don't remember them now because what happened afterwards knocked everything else right out of my head. I was just thinking maybe she'd get the Nobel Prize when she was about fourteen, when the door of my room opened. There wasn't even a knock, even though the single most important rule in our family is that everybody has to knock before opening a closed door. It was Grandpa.

At first I didn't notice anything wrong except that he had forgotten to knock and I was just about to say something about it when he started talking.

"Sophie," he said, "where's Mama? Why didn't she fix me any oatmeal this morning? I'm hungry!"

Of course Grandpa knows perfectly well my name is Kerry. The only Sophie I have ever even heard of is Great Aunt Sophie, Grandpa's older sister who died years and years ago. But at the moment, I didn't even remember that. I was just surprised and kind of confused. Then I saw that Grandpa was barefoot, but he had on a bow tie. He hates ties, and it's always a big deal to get him to put on a tie when we go someplace dressy. It wasn't much, and Jeannie probably didn't notice it at all, but I knew it meant trouble.

Jeannie looked at me funny, but I could tell she thought it was some kind of game between Grandpa and me, so I pretended it was and went along with him.

"I'm supposed to fix your oatmeal," I told him. "Go get your shoes on and your breakfast will be ready in no time."

I sort of pushed him out of my room and toward the stairs. When he was safely on his way down, I ran back and told Jeannie to wait for me while I fixed Grandpa some instant oatmeal.

She started to ask me something, but I shut the door practically in her face and went after Grandpa, who was going down the stairs very slowly, holding onto the railing with both hands. I sort of helped him along and got him into his room.

"Sophie," he kept saying over and over, "where's Mama? I'm hungry! Where's Mama?" I was wracking my brain trying to remember anything I could about Sophie—by this time I'd remembered who she was—but I never knew much about his family.

"Mama will be here soon," I told him. "Just put on your shoes and I'll bring your oatmeal right in here. You can have breakfast in your room."

Jeannie came into the kitchen as I was stirring the boiling water into the oatmeal. "What's going on?" she asked.

I don't know what came over me, because Jeannie was only asking a perfectly reasonable question. She didn't know what was happening, and she is, after all, my best friend in the world. But I just yelled, "Mind your own business! I told you to wait upstairs!" Then I grabbed the bowl and a spoon and went to Grandpa's room.

When I came back Jeannie was sitting at the kitchen table with her journal. You have to hand it to her. If somebody had just said to me what I'd said to her, I'd have picked up my things and gone home. Even though I never expect to see her again, I know she's what a real friend is supposed to be. At least as a hermit I'll know that once upon a time I had a true friend!

"Something's wrong!" she said. "I started reading you my journal without even giving you a chance to tell me what happened here while I was gone. What's the matter?"

I don't remember what I told her, but I tried to make out that Grandpa and I were just playing a game we'd made up and I was embarrassed to have her there because it seemed silly. I said the only thing that had happened while she was gone was that I'd decided to be the butterfly champion of the world and had fallen in love, so we'd better go to the pool where she could see me swim and meet my boyfriend. I can hardly believe I told her that last part, but all I wanted right then was to get out of the house and away from Grandpa before he came back out and started calling me Sophie again.

I don't think she really believed me about the game with Grandpa, but she acted like she did, so I ran up and got into my bathing suit as fast as I could and we went to the park. Mom was supposed to be home from a sales meeting almost any time, so I figured there would be somebody at home by the time Grandpa finished his oatmeal and came out again.

We went to the pool and I swam a couple of

lengths of the butterfly stroke, not as fast as my record time, but not too bad either. Then I did two widths underwater and by that time I'd almost forgotten about Grandpa except for a kind of achy feeling in the bottom of my stomach. Jeannie pretended to be very impressed at my speed and whistled the "Star Spangled Banner" when I came out of the pool to let me know I'd won a gold medal. Kevin was busy with his beginners, so I whispered that he was the great love of my life and Jeannie cracked up. She was making such a scene that I had to get her away from the pool before he noticed us.

"He's at least sixteen. At least!" she kept saying as I shoved her toward my favorite spot under an oak tree. "You've got to be kidding!"

She finally settled down and I got her to forget Kevin long enough to read some more from her journal. Then the disaster happened. If I close my eyes right this minute I can see it all over again. Maybe I'll never be able to close my eyes again! I was leaning against the tree, listening to her read and sort of staring out over the pool where Kevin was trying to get a little kid to let go of the gutter, when I saw Grandpa coming through the gate in the pool fence. He was wearing nothing but his trousers, with the legs rolled up to his knees. He looked like he was looking for somebody, so I stood up to wave at him. Jeannie stopped reading and looked, too. Then I realized that he was crying. Not just a little, like you might expect a grownup to cry, but bawling hard—like a little kid. I started toward him, and even over all the noise of the pool I could hear him bawling and calling, "Sophie! Sophie!" He was getting close to the deep end of the pool.

I started to run toward him, but he was too far away, and he just stepped right off the edge of the pool into the water.

Now if there is one thing in the world my grandpa knows, it's how to swim. But after he stepped off the edge of the pool, he didn't swim. He came up once, still crying and sort of coughing, and then went down again. He didn't even try to swim. He just sank right down to the bottom. I don't think I'll be able to forget it as long as I live. First there was his white hair coming up and then he went down, his body looking so small and so bony. I screamed for Kevin and jumped in after Grandpa.

From then on everything is a blur. Kevin and the other lifeguard and I got him out of the water so fast he didn't even need mouth-to-mouth. We got a towel over him and I was crying and Jeannie was there and then she must have gone for my mother, because pretty soon Mom was there, too. Kevin kept having to shove people back out of the way. The shock must have snapped Grandpa out of it because by the time Mom came he was sitting up and complaining about all the fuss. In all the blur of what was happening then, there is only one moment that stands out clear to me now. It was when Grandpa first opened his eyes after he was pulled out of the pool.

I was holding his hand, and for just one second, before he got mad at all the people clustering around him, he looked scared and sort of lost. I mean it was Grandpa, not that crazy person who'd been calling me Sophie. It was Grandpa all right. It was like he was waking up from a nightmare and not sure where he was. He looked at me as if he needed me to help him somehow. Then he sort of shook his head and began hollering for people to get back and let him alone.

After Mom got there things calmed down a little and we got him home and into his bed. Jeannie came home with us and offered to help if she could, but Mom wasn't talking much, and I told her to go home and I'd call her later. But I won't. I don't want to see her, or Kevin, or anybody else who was at the pool today ever again.

Mom called Dad and he came straight home from work and they're downstairs right now arguing. Mom's been crying and Dad's been yelling and Grandpa's asleep. Matt isn't home yet, so he doesn't even know what's happened.

I've been trying not to remember that moment when Grandpa looked so lost, but I can't help it. I wonder if you can be going crazy and know you are going crazy and not want to be going crazy. I wonder if it's like being in the middle of a dream and knowing it's a dream and wanting to wake up but not being able to open your eyes.

And how could Grandpa show me that trilobite fossil one day and start calling me Sophie the next? I haven't told Mom about that yet, but I'll have to pretty soon. Dr. Harris said he'd come by after office hours, and I guess I'll have to tell him, too. But I don't think I can tell them about the other time in the backyard.

TUESDAY, JULY 29, 4:00 p.m.

Everybody knows now that Grandpa is crazy. Nobody has used that word, but it's the same thing. I've spent the whole day in bed because the only way I can stay in my room without a lot of hassle is if I'm sick. So I've been sick—a headache. Mom gets these really terrible sinus headaches, so she doesn't ask questions when somebody has a headache. She just gives them aspirin and leaves them alone.

Jeannie came over this morning. I heard her downstairs asking how Grandpa was and if I could come over to her house. Mom told her that Grandpa was going to be fine and that I was in bed with a headache but I'd probably be better this afternoon, and Jeannie went home.

Dr. Harris came over last night after supper. Grandpa was still in his room, so the doctor went in there to look at him. By that time Matt was home and had been told that Grandpa had fallen into the pool. But nobody knew the whole story, even then. After Dr. Harris had been with Grandpa for a while Mom called Matt and me into the living room. Dad was there, sitting in his chair and looking kind of angry. Mom's eyes were red from crying, but she seemed to be okay. Matt and I sat down, but everything was uncomfortable between us—like the time we'd gone to church with Aunt Joan and nobody but her had known when to kneel or when to stand up or what. I kept watching Mom and Dad and wondering what they wanted us there for, but they seemed to have forgotten we were there.

Finally Dr. Harris came in with a big, fake, cheerful smile. "Your father is going to be all right," he told Mom. "He's a little disoriented, but there are apparently no complications from the accident. I've given him a sedative and he should sleep through the night."

Mom tried to smile back at Dr. Harris, but it didn't look too convincing. "I can't understand it," she said. "He's such a fine swimmer!"

Dr. Harris turned off his smile then, and I could tell he was going to say something real.

"Have you noticed any changes in his behavior lately?" he asked.

I looked at Matt, who didn't seem to know what was going on. I guess he didn't remember the morning with the inside-out pants. Nobody said a word.

"He seems to be physically fine, but a little out of touch. Have you noticed any memory losses or anything of that nature?"

Dad frowned and shook his head, but I noticed that Mom was fiddling with her rings and not looking at anybody. She looked the way I was feeling—like she knew some things she didn't want anybody else to know.

I remembered, then, the look Grandpa had given me when we got him out of the pool, and I decided the doctor should know what I knew at least. If anyone could help Grandpa, he could. So I told them about his calling me Sophie and crying before he fell in the pool. Then I told them about the day with the pants and the hat. When I finished Mom was crying again. I looked at Dad and he didn't look angry anymore. He was watching Mom and even though she was the one who was crying, I couldn't tell which of them felt worse.

"Sophie was Dad's sister," Mom said finally. Her voice was so low it was hard to hear. "She took care of him after his mother died. He was only four then, and the youngest of the five children. Sophie was the oldest—twelve, I guess. She took over the family and cared for all the children—and Grandfather, too. Sophie never married and I was still little myself when she died. I don't remember her, and Dad has hardly spoken of her since the funeral. I guess Sophie's death was like losing his mother a second time."

Dr. Harris nodded. "This isn't so unusual for a man of your father's age," he told Mom. "He has temporarily lost track of time. This afternoon he must have been four years old again, reliving the confusion and pain of his mother's death. Kerry may look very much like Sophie did then. She's just about the right age. He thought she was Sophie and went looking for her. That would also explain why he didn't swim to the side when he fell into the pool. At four, he wouldn't have been able to swim."

I didn't wait to hear any more. I just got up and ran up to my room. I knew Dr. Harris was right. It was not Grandpa who kept asking for his mama. That's why I had been so sure he was crazy. There had been something so strange about the way he talked. And now I knew what it was. I wasn't hearing an eighty-year-old man, I was hearing a four-year-old. The kid Grandpa had been in 1902. And he thought I was Sophie—a person who'd been dead since my mother was a little girl. It gave me the creeps, but it made me sad, too. So sad it was like I had an enormous rock in my stomach. All I wanted to do was go to sleep and get away from it.

Mom came up to my room this morning and told me that Grandpa isn't really crazy (only she said "mentally ill" because she hates the word "crazy"), just old. She says the trouble will come and go, and that mostly he'll probably be his usual self.

I asked her what we were going to do about Grandpa and then I wished I hadn't. She didn't cry. I think she cried so much last night that she doesn't have any tears left. But she sat down on the edge of my bed and got a kind of faraway look in her eyes. She said they hadn't decided yet. Then she just sat there for a while, not saying anything.

It was then that I realized something for the very first time. It's really dumb, since Grandpa has lived with us since I can remember, and since I've known the whole time that he is Mom's father. But right then I understood what that really means—that Grandpa is her dad. That he means to her what Dad means to me. I tried to imagine what I would feel like if Dad suddenly started acting crazy and then I knew why she argued with Dad about nursing homes and why she had cried so much last night. She was sitting on the edge of my bed wondering whether she would have to have her father locked up or not. I don't think I've ever felt closer to Mom than I did then. I wanted to tell her how I felt, but I couldn't think what to say. Finally she rubbed her forehead and stood up. Then she patted my head sort of absentmindedly and went downstairs. I wondered if we would always miss the chance to let each other know we understood like we had just then.

I didn't go down for lunch—just had some crackers I keep in my room in case I get hungry in the night. I didn't feel much like eating anyway. Most of the time I've been hibernating I've been thinking about Sophie. She was only twelve years old when her mother died. I'll be twelve in October. Sophie had four little brothers and sisters to take care of, and her father, too. I tried to imagine how it must have been, but I couldn't. Picture me, Kerry Warren, age eleven-almost-twelve, taking care of four kids and Dad. It would be dry cereal for breakfast and grilled cheese for lunch and dinner every single day. I can't even fix decent pancakes from a box! I guess I could probably learn to cook some other things, but what would it be like to take care of the kids, too? Mom won't even let me babysit till I'm fourteen.

Then I remembered that Sophie couldn't have given anybody pancakes from a box—they didn't have mixes in those days. And no Cheerios either. I wondered what else they didn't have in 1902. No washers and dryers.

How did she do the laundry? And no permanent press clothes either. How did she have time for school? The more I thought about Sophie, the more impossible it all became.

I wish Grandpa had told me about her before. I'd never tried to imagine what it must have been like when he was little, or what his family was like. I never even knew his mother died when he was four. It's as if Grandpa's always been an old man. For one thing, if I think of him as a little boy, my mother, who has always been a grownup, completely disappears. She wasn't even born until he was thirty-four. So when he was four, that was still thirty years before Mom was born! It's mind-boggling.

I spent half an hour working out all the dates and ages this afternoon. Grandpa was the same age when Mom was born that Mom was when I was born. She was the youngest in her family, with Aunt Joan and Uncle Dan before her. I can't understand why nobody has ever talked about our family before. It isn't just Grandpa I don't know about. It's Mom and Aunt Joan and Uncle Dan and Grandma and Dad and his family, too! They must have a million stories they could tell about when they were little, but they never have.

I have decided to get well and come out of hibernation. I want to find out more about Aunt Sophie. And everybody else. Grandpa showed me some old photo albums once a long time ago and I glanced through them just to make him happy. I don't remember much about what I saw except that there were a lot of really stern-looking men with long mustaches and women with high-collared dresses and their hair all on top of their heads. I remember that the little kids were all in dresses—even the boys. But since I didn't know any of the people, I didn't care very much. I guess Grandpa realized I wasn't interested because he didn't tell me about any of the pictures either.

But I want to get a look at Sophie. I hope there's a picture of her when she was twelve, because I just have to see if I really do look like her. And I want to see if you could tell, just looking at her, that this was the kind of person who could manage a house and four kids and her father when she still must have felt like a little kid herself. And a little kid whose mother had just died all of a sudden, too.

Maybe Mom will be able to find the albums for me. I don't think I want to risk asking Grandpa about Sophie. And I'll have to call Jeannie after all. She'll really want to know about Sophie!

TUESDAY, JULY 29, 10:00 p.m.

Supper was terrible. Mom and Dad weren't talking, Grandpa had eaten in his room and was in there with the television on, and Matt started in about this baseball game he is going to play in at the park on Saturday. He was acting as big and important as he always does about baseball, expecting everybody to be impressed with how great he is, only nobody was listening. He kept on for a while, bragging how everybody says he's the best pitcher and how with him on the mound Fletcher Park can't help but beat Jackson Park. After a while he sort of ran down—like a music box nobody'd remembered to wind.

From then on, he just sat there, stuffing food into his mouth and staring at his plate. I don't know whether it's worse when he's being quiet or worse when he's talking about things nobody else wants to hear about, but I can't understand how he can be part of this family and how he could have listened to Dr. Harris and still feel like bragging about his dumb old baseball game. It's like his world has no connection with our world at all. Anyway, this is probably the first time in his life Dad didn't get all excited when Matt was telling how good he was at something, so he must have known something was wrong in our world. He went off without even asking about dessert—there wasn't any anyway—but I don't think he was feeling rotten for the same reason the rest of us were. I can hardly believe that a person who is almost fourteen can be so out of it!

They didn't ask me about my headache so I guess they knew I'd been faking. When Mom started to clear the table I helped and she didn't seem to notice me. If nothing else had told me how bad things were, that would have. I never do anything with the supper dishes unless somebody tells me to. I figure that's a job for Mom or Dad—I keep my room clean and dust on Saturday. Of course I end up doing the supper dishes a lot too, because they tell me to a lot, even though Dad is the one who's really supposed to do them. Even Matt gets told to do dishes pretty often. But this time it was like I was invisible or something. Dad went out to the kitchen too and started to rinse the dishes while Mom put away the food, and then I wasn't so invisible anymore, because they told me to go up to my room. I figured they were going to talk about Grandpa again and didn't want me listening, because ordinarily they'd have been glad to have me help. Anyway, I hadn't called Jeannie yet, so I didn't mind being told to leave.

It took me a pretty long time to get upstairs to the phone in their room because I sort of walked slow and listened as long as I could. And I stopped at Grandpa's door to see if his TV was still on, so he wouldn't hear what they were saying. He had it up good and loud, and it was a good thing, because they were back on nursing homes again. Maybe they still don't understand about Grandpa after all. He won't be able to go to a plain nursing home—he isn't sick like with pneumonia or a broken leg or something like that. He's crazy.

If he started doing what he did that morning in the yard right in front of everybody at some nursing home, they'd send him away fast enough. And then I started wondering what they do with crazy people in an asylum. I guess they don't use straitjackets much anymore, but they must have to keep people from getting out and doing crazy things. There would be bars on the windows and locks on the doors, I guess. Like prison.

By the time I'd thought of that, I was upstairs and couldn't hear anything from the kitchen except a kind of muttering as they talked. But I was glad to be alone, because thinking about Grandpa locked in a room in some insane asylum really scared me. I sat on Mom and Dad's bed for a long time, looking at the phone and thinking about how Grandpa would feel if he couldn't go to the park or walk or jog or look for rocks or play shuffleboard with Mr. Buhler. Even if he hadn't had much to do lately, he could go where he wanted to go. And I wondered if crazy people are allowed to have their families visit them, and if they are, if I'd be old enough. Regular hospitals don't let people visit till they're fourteen. And that would be stupid because that would mean Matt could visit Grandpa before I could, and he doesn't even have sense enough to see what's happening.

After that I don't remember what I thought about, but it was a long time before I remembered to call Jeannie and tell her about Sophie, and even then I couldn't feel as excited about her as I had before supper. Jeannie said she'd come over in the morning. So I'm out of hibernation and I have a friend again. But I won't go back to the park. Or swim in the pool. Not ever.

WEDNESDAY, JULY 30, noon

Grandpa was at breakfast this morning, pretty much his old self except that sometimes he would stop in the middle of chewing a mouthful of scrambled eggs and stare off into space. Then he'd sort of shake his head and start chewing again. But it wasn't like he was being crazy, just like he was thinking about something. I thought of asking him about his albums, but I didn't, for fear it would upset him.

Dad was talking about a job he was planning to do at the office today and Mom was only partly listening, but she seemed to be in better shape than she was yesterday. Matt wasn't up yet. "Don't eat too big a breakfast before practice," Grandpa said when he noticed me packing away my plateful of eggs. "You can't swim on a full stomach!"

I swallowed the egg in my mouth and tried to think what to tell him. He thought he'd be coaching me today, and nobody knew I'd decided never to go back to the pool. "I can't swim today, Grandpa," I said, trying like mad to come up with a good enough reason. "I—uh—I don't feel very well today. I had a headache all day yesterday, and I don't feel like swimming today." There was a long silence and I went on eating, staring down at my plate. I could feel everybody looking at me, but I pretended not to notice. Then Grandpa gave a sort of a chuckle and I looked up just in time to see him wink at Mom.

"Never press a lady who says no," he said, and winked at Mom again. I choked and felt my face getting hot.

"Mom—" I said, but she shook her head. I guess she was right. There was no use trying to straighten it out. At least now he wouldn't expect to go to the pool with me for a while. Dad got up to go to work and gave Mom a hug—something he doesn't always remember to do in the morning. Grandpa didn't seem to notice.

But then Mom told Dad she was going to stay home to clean the house. Grandpa had just started to get up from the table when she said that. He sat back down and looked at her. She was talking to Dad and didn't see the look Grandpa gave her. My mother has never stayed home from work just to clean house in her whole life. Our house gets cleaned in the evenings or on Saturday mornings when Matt and I can help. Mom is not one to make a project of cleaning house—especially on a work day. A person would have to be a whole lot crazier than Grandpa is to buy that story.

Grandpa did get up then and said he would go find Mr. Buhler and play some chess. When Mom and I were alone in the kitchen I almost told her what a mistake it had been to pretend she was staying home to clean house, but she was sitting at the table with her second cup of coffee, looking tired, so I let it go. I put my dishes in the sink and asked if she knew where Grandpa's albums were.

"What do you want those for?" she asked.

"I want to see if there are any pictures of Sophie," I told her and she nodded.

"Try his closet shelves. I don't think he'd mind."

Grandpa's shelves are pretty crowded. He's got all the stuff he saved after Grandma died in boxes piled halfway up to the ceiling. But the albums were easy to find. They were right on the top where he could get them if he wanted to look at them. There were three—big, heavy books with padded covers and faded gold lettering that said "Family Album" on the fronts. One was dark red velvet and the other two were black—silk maybe. I took them up to my room and closed the door. Jeannie would be over soon, I knew, but I couldn't wait for her. I wanted to get a look at Sophie.

You could sure tell that Kodak and Polaroid weren't around in those days. There weren't any pictures that looked like any of the pictures of us. We have this big box of snapshots that Mom keeps saying she's going to organize and put into albums some day. I don't think she ever will, but even if she did, they wouldn't be anything like Grandpa's albums. Each page is made of heavy cardboard with a hole in the middle for a picture. And all the pictures are really formal—more like the studio picture Mom and Dad had done for their anniversary than like our family snapshots. Most of the pictures are of one or two people. They are dressed in fancy clothes and either standing or sitting in an elegant chair in front of a painted scene. And nobody is smiling. There are babies in some of the pictures, with white ruffly gowns about fifty times too long for them and some little kids in pleated dresses with belts that look as if they were made for somebody six inches bigger around the middle than they are. Most of the girls have dresses that reach the tops of their shoes, and their hair is worn long, with ribbons. Most of the boys are in shorter dresses with long black stockings showing.

The shoes surprised me most. I knew people used to wear high button shoes, but I guess I'd never seen any before. They go clear up above the ankles with tiny little buttons all up one side, and even the littlest kids are wearing them. It must have taken about an hour to get them on, and kids would have to have help. I wondered if Sophie had to button everybody's shoes every morning.

There are pictures that were taken outside too, but even those are stiff and posed and nobody seems to be smiling. There is one picture of about fifty women all in rows on some bleachers with one man right in the middle. He's sitting there with the meanest look on his face—what you can see of his face behind his big, droopy mustache and pointy beard. I don't know what that picture is about, but I don't like that man. The women around him look even gloomier than the ones in the other pictures. And right down at the bottom of that one are a whole bunch of girls, some of them no older than I am. They look saddest of all. I decided that was a picture I wanted to ask someone about, so I put a piece of paper in to mark it before I went on looking.

Before I'd finished the first album, Jeannie knocked on my door. I must have been concentrating on the pictures pretty hard, because I hadn't heard the back doorbell. But I still hadn't found anyone I could be sure was Sophie.

I told Jeannie all about Sophie taking over the whole family when she was twelve, and she was as interested in her as I thought she'd be.

"But we've got to organize," she said. "Get some paper. First we'll mark all the pictures we're interested in—all the ones with a girl about the right age, or the ones we want to know something special about. Then we'll do a diagram of the pictures so we can fill in names later."

Jeannie's ideas usually work, so I got the paper and we started. She figured we could ask Grandpa about the pictures we wanted to know about, and then fill in the names that way. The only trouble with her idea is that I don't want to ask Grandpa about the pictures. But I'm not quite ready to tell Jeannie everything about Grandpa yet either. I guess maybe Mom will know about some of the people.

I was glad to find out that Jeannie didn't know any more than I did about what life was like back then. We tried to imagine getting up in the morning and putting on all the clothes they wore—and buttoning up those shoes. She said they had button hooks to help with their shoes, but she couldn't believe a hook would be all that much help. A kid was probably in the sixth grade before he could do up his own shoes! And we decided they must have been awfully hot in the summertime. We found one outside picture where a little girl was barefooted—but even in that picture most of the other kids were wearing long black stockings.

I found a picture of a little boy I thought might be Grandpa, but I couldn't be sure. Several of the kids looked a little like him, but I've never seen him without his mustache or with hair any color except white, so it's hard to tell.

We finally finished the diagrams of the pictures we thought might have Sophie or Grandpa or his parents in them, but even Jeannie had to admit we hadn't learned much. She has to visit her aunt this afternoon, so I think I'm going to see if I can find any books around the house about what it was like to live eighty years ago. I want to find out more about what it was like to be Sophie!

THURSDAY, JULY 31, 11:00 a.m.

When I woke up this morning it was still early and nobody was up. For a long time I stayed in bed thinking about Sophie, and then I decided to pretend I was Sophie and fix everybody breakfast. It's about time I learned to fix something—eggs at least. I figured there was bound to be a cookbook in the kitchen that would tell me what to do, and I ought to be able to follow directions. Anyway, Mom could use the rest. So I got dressed as quietly as I could and went downstairs. But I never got a chance to try the eggs. When I got to the kitchen I couldn't even go in. All the lower cupboard doors were hanging open and the pots and pans were piled in the middle of the floor. The pantry was open too, and almost everything had been dumped. Boxes of cereal had been opened and sprinkled over the piles of pans. A bag of flour was lying, split open, where it had been dropped. Flour was everywhere. Cans were stacked in towers, and some of the towers had been knocked over. There was a can of fruit cocktail in the middle of the kitchen doorway and a can of tomatoes in the hall.

I just stood there, staring at the mess for the longest time—it was such a surprise. Through all of it there were bare footprints in the flour and there was no problem figuring out whose they were. For a minute I was afraid he might have gone out somewhere, but then I noticed white footprints leading out of the kitchen and down the hall toward his room. At least he was safe inside. I tiptoed around the mess and checked the back door to be sure it was locked—for some reason I wanted there to be a lock between Grandpa and the outside world right then, even if it was on the inside, and even if Grandpa could open it perfectly well.

I thought of trying to clean everything up before anybody got up so I wouldn't have to tell Mom, but it was no use. Half the stuff from the pantry was ruined and she'd notice that right away, even if I could get the mess cleaned up before she came down. So I wiped my feet with my hands so I wouldn't track flour upstairs and went to wake Mom and Dad. I realized now that no matter how much we loved Grandpa, we were going to have to do something soon.

Mom and Dad came down together, and when they got to the kitchen door they didn't say anything. Dad put his arm around Mom and she leaned her head on his shoulder and they just looked. I guess I was sort of expecting Mom to cry again, but after a couple of minutes she began to laugh. Then Dad started laughing, and I decided my whole family was going crazy! That mess was no laughing matter as far as I could see. But they kept laughing harder and harder until Mom was wiping tears from her eyes.

Then Matt came up. He must have been sleeping in the basement. He looked at Mom and Dad and then he looked at the mess and then he looked back at Mom and Dad and I think he finally realized that something awful was happening to our family.

Mom sat down at the kitchen table and Dad stood beside her with one hand on her back—like the couples in those old photographs, except they were still laughing like crazy. Mom finally caught her breath. "Matt, by rights, you ought to clean this up!"

Matt got this stricken look on his face and I

thought he'd take off back to the basement, but she went on before he had a chance to run.

"When you were eighteen months old you did almost exactly the same thing. I came downstairs to fix breakfast and this is what I found. Except that right in the middle of the mess was you, covered with flour, curled among the pots and pans in your fuzzy blue pajamas, sound asleep. We didn't even know you could get out of your crib yet! Your father cleaned it up that time, because I was pregnant with Kerry and couldn't stand the sight of all that food at that hour of the morning." She started to laugh again.

Dad had got hold of himself by then. "Okay, you two, let's get busy. We've got some cleaning up to do!"

I headed for the pantry, but Matt started to object, and Dad's voice changed very fast. It came out low and very clear. "You are a part of this family, Matthew Warren, and it's about time you got that into your head. We are in this together, whatever it means. Now get the broom!"

Afterwards, even though it was only Thursday, Mom made a big Sunday morning kind of breakfast—Dad called his office to tell them he'd be late—and we had a kind of celebration. It was really weird. Grandpa came out just as Mom was starting breakfast and acted like nothing had happened. I guess he didn't remember. Anyway, we were all sort of silly from cleaning up. Matt and Dad were joking around with each other like they used to before Matt started hiding out in the basement. It was like a flashback in the movies—back to a time when we were all together, before everybody got so busy with other people. We really were a family again.

Maybe the weirdest thing about it was the way Mom was acting. All of a sudden she was smiling and laughing. The grumps and worries she's been having since Grandpa fell in the pool just seemed to have gone away, as if the mess he'd made in the kitchen had solved the problem instead of making it worse. Sometimes there is no use trying to understand the adult mind, I guess. After I bothered around about it for a few minutes, I gave up and just ate and had fun. It was the best breakfast we've had in a long time. I read a book once where the girl gives her days different grades. I don't know about the whole day, but breakfast was definitely an A+.

Afterwards Dad went to work and Matt went off to David Melkerson's and Grandpa said he would have to take a long walk to work off all the calories in that breakfast. He asked me to go along, but I said I'd help Mom with the dishes. "Sure are a lot of changes going on around here," he said as he left. I wondered if he knew that the changes had to do with him.

While we were doing the dishes I asked Mom if she'd ever really looked at Grandpa's albums before. She stopped washing the frying pan for a minute and looked out the window without saying anything and I thought she was seeing something out in the backyard and got worried again. But then she went back to scrubbing. "I've looked at all of them, but it's been a long, long time."

"Well, it's kind of hard to tell anything," I told her, "because I don't know who any of the people in the pictures are. I mean, I guess Grandpa and Sophie and the others are all in them, but I don't know which ones they are. There are an awful lot of people. Would you know them?"

Mom let the dishwater out of the sink and dried her hands. "I tell you what" she said in that voice she uses when she's suggesting a picnic or a trip to an amusement park or something. "I'll finish drying these while you go up and get the albums. I'm not going to work again today, so we'll just take some time and look at them together. I don't know how much I'll remember, but I know I'll recognize some of them. It's about time I looked at those pictures again."

So for the next hour Mom and I sat at the kitchen table with Grandpa's albums. It turned out she knew a whole bunch of the people—

Grandpa's mother and father and all the brothers and sisters. She had known most of them when she was little. She didn't do so well with cousins and uncles and aunts—there hadn't been too much visiting among the families. I filled in names on the diagrams, and by the time we were done, most of the blanks I really cared about were filled in and I was feeling pretty good about it.

I was disappointed that there wasn't a single picture of Sophie when she was twelve, though. I guess nobody was in the mood to have a picture taken just after my great-grandmother died. There was a picture of all of them when Grandpa was a baby, though. He was one of the babies in the long white dresses. The picture was of his mother and all five kids—Grandpa's christening picture. Sophie must have been eight, and even though I got a mirror from Mom's purse and looked at myself and then at Sophie and then back at myself again, I couldn't see any resemblance at all. Mom said she could. I think I'll try to find a picture of me when I was eight and compare it to Sophie. Maybe then I'll be able to see it.

Grandpa's mother was really something! There she is, sitting in that big chair with Grandpa in her lap in his dress and ruffly cap with four other kids standing around her and she looks so young you'd think she was posing for a prom queen picture or something. Of all the women in the albums, she looks the most real. I mean she doesn't look stiff and dead and old-fashioned the way the rest of them do. I can look at her and imagine that the picture was taken yesterday—in a costume. She looks as if she could walk into the room with you any minute. Mostly, I guess, she looks soft. And round. Sophie is standing next to her with her hands on her shoulder and she's the only one in the picture except Grandpa who isn't looking right out at the camera. She is looking at her mother.

Sophie isn't soft, though. She's kind of wiry, and maybe even a little mean looking. I'll bet if she were still alive she'd be even more worried about physical fitness than Grandpa.

Then there's the two boys, Jonathan and Henry, both of them in sailor suits with dutch boy haircuts, and a little bitty girl sort of leaning on her mother's leg. She looks like she's just barely big enough to walk.

After I'd filled in all the names on the diagram of that picture, I put a big star on it. It may not be the right year, but it shows all the kids Sophie had to take care of and the mother she had to live without, too. It's the picture I most want to get to know. I got the feeling, looking at that picture, that the more I look at those albums, the more I'll get to know those kids. After a while, I had trouble remembering that the people I was looking at are almost all dead now.

There were pictures in the last album of the kids grown up, too. Sophie didn't change all that much—just got taller and even more wiry. Grandpa was the best looking of them, with his dark mustache and all that dark hair. It's turned white over the years, but he sure hasn't lost much of it. It's fun to see how they all changed as they grew up, but it's the pictures of them as kids that I like best and that I feel I could get to know.

After we'd finished with all three albums, Mom went off to the park to find Grandpa and walk him home. I knew she was worried about letting him walk in the park alone, but when she left she seemed to be looking forward to walking with him. She said she hadn't been to the park in a long time and it would do her some good. Talk about weird! From the moment she started laughing at the mess in the kitchen this morning, my mother has been like a different person.

Jeannie's coming over after lunch and I'm going to tell her who everybody is in the pictures. I can't wait. I don't know how to explain it or anything—it's almost like science fiction—but I feel like I can almost get inside those pictures, and that the people in them are strangers but not strangers. Maybe Jeannie will understand what I mean.

THURSDAY, JULY 31, bedtime

Jeannie and I are going to do a project. She's going to write a historical novel—mostly about Sophie—and I'm going to be her research assistant. She says a novel shouldn't be too hard to write if you get organized well enough first and get all the facts together. Besides, we have the main part of the story already, so we don't have to think that up. I'm supposed to do most of the research, and we're going to the library tomorrow to get started. I sort of like the sound of "research assistant," but I haven't told Jeannie yet that I don't know the first thing about doing research. I figure we'll start out together and I'll find out how to do it as we go along. There are lots of things I want to know about those days.

That picture of all the women and the one man turns out to be a picture of the workers at a factory. And their boss. The little kids across the bottom of the picture worked at the factory too, all day every day. It's no wonder they look so gloomy. Mom says kids didn't have to go to school back then—in fact most kids were needed to help at home, like Sophie, or to earn money, like the kids at the factory. We learned about child labor laws in school, but I didn't think much about what they meant. I can hardly imagine what it would be like to work in a factory. Mom thinks one of the girls in that picture is a cousin of Grandpa's and that Sophie would have worked there too if she hadn't had to take care of the family. I wonder which Sophie would have wanted to do if she'd been able to choose.

But when I remember the look on her face in the picture with her mother, I guess she'd rather have had her mother alive and worked in a factory than have her mother die and leave her to manage the kids. My great-grandmother looks like a mother you'd miss an awful lot.

I don't know how I'd get along without Jeannie. Sometimes she makes me feel pretty dumb, but she says that a person on the outside can understand things a person all mixed up with a problem doesn't even see. I finally told her all about Grandpa—everything—and how Mom changed this morning when she started laughing at the mess he'd made. Jeannie thought about it for a minute—only about a minute, when I've been thinking about it all day!

"I bet I know!" she said. "If Matt did the same thing when he was a baby, the mess didn't seem so bad."

With my usual perception, I sat there looking blank. "See, she's been upset because her father has been acting crazy and doing all these weird things. But when she remembered what Matt was like when he was a baby, and the things he did, then what your grandfather's been doing didn't seem so weird anymore. Do you suppose Matt ever wandered away from the yard when he was little and got into trouble—like when your grandpa fell in the pool?"

I remembered a story Mom told me once about *me.* "One day when I was supposed to be taking a nap, I got up and went outside. I went down the street in my underwear and went right into somebody's house. Mom said she was so embarrassed, she didn't know what to say when this lady she didn't even know came up to the door with me and asked if I was hers. I had gone right into her kitchen and taken an apple out of her refrigerator. She didn't have any kids of her own and was really steamed. Mom offered to pay for the apple, but the lady told her if she couldn't take better care of her children than that, she shouldn't have any. I guess it must have been a long time before Mom felt like laughing about that!"

"Exactly!" Jeannie said, and even I saw what she was getting at. Then Jeannie did one of the kinds of things she's always doing that would make some people think *she's* crazy. Right in the middle of this perfectly reasonable conversation we were having, she jumped up off my bed, dumping all the diagrams and pictures on the floor, and ran out of the room. If you didn't know her like I do, you would probably run after her to find out what was wrong. But I just picked things up and waited. There are times when I think maybe Jeannie isn't just smart. Maybe she's a genius. I've heard that geniuses do crazy things when they're working on a discovery. Anyway, I've learned just to wait her out and see what she's up to. Most of the time it's worth it.

This time she was back in two minutes with our copy of Shakespeare's *Complete Works* from the living room. "Have you read *As You Like It?*" she asked.

She knows the answer to that one. One of our biggest arguments is about Shakespeare. I can't stand the way all the people in his plays talk; I can't figure out what they're saying. But she thinks practically everything worth saying or even thinking is somewhere in Shakespeare if you can find it. I didn't tell her that Shakespeare hadn't ever said a single thing about my grandfather falling into a swimming pool, in case she was going to prove I was wrong.

"There's a famous speech that starts, 'All the world's a stage.' "

I felt better. "I know that speech!" I said. "Miss Schreiber made us learn that for dramatics. But I don't see what that has to do with Grandpa."

Jeannie was thumbing through the pages. "Not the beginning. There's a lot more to that speech. It's the one about the seven ages of man! He tells about how a person is first a baby and then a schoolboy and then—I don't know—a lover, I think. Anyway, there are seven of them altogether . . ." She stopped and ran her finger down a page. "Here it is! Listen. 'The sixth age shifts into the lean and slipper'd pantaloon,' then there's some more, then, 'his big manly voice turning again toward childish treble, pipes and whistles in his sound. Last scene of all, that ends this strange eventful history,' now this is it—'is second childishness, and mere oblivion sans teeth, sans eyes, sans taste, sans everything.' There. Your Grandpa isn't crazy. He's in the Seventh Age! It's perfectly natural."

"And that's what Mom found out this morning when she saw that mess!"

"Sure. If she could live through that kind of thing when Matt and you were little, she ought to be able to live through it now with her father. And probably he had to live through it with her, you know."

"I guess that's another part of being a family," I said. I had to sit there and think about it for a while, but it made sense. Maybe Jeannie's right about Shakespeare after all. It's pretty incredible that somebody who lived four hundred years ago could say something about my grandfather. But I didn't make a big fuss over her finding that quotation. I think it's better for her character if I don't let her know how smart she is sometimes. Anyway, it was time for her to go home, so we put back the *Complete Works* and arranged to go to the library in the morning.

I've been thinking about that quotation ever since she read it, and about Mom and Grandpa and about me wandering into that lady's house. It isn't Grandpa's fault that he's acting crazy any more than it was my fault when I went into her house. And if she had understood anything about children, she wouldn't have been so upset. If people understood about the Seventh Age, they wouldn't be so upset when somebody starts acting like Grandpa either, I guess. Mom always says that she had a hard time when we were little until she stopped worrying about what other people thought about us. When she finally realized that it didn't matter what everybody else thought as long as she knew us and took care of us the best way she could and loved us, she could finally relax about having little kids who sometimes threw tantrums in stores and stuff.

I wish I were a better person. I love Grandpa, and I think I understand about the Seventh Age, so I shouldn't worry about what other people think. But every time I remember him coming to the pool, I know I just can't go back there and face everybody again.

There's something else I've been thinking about the Seventh Age, too. It must be a terrible thing to have happen to you. "Sans" means without. I checked after Jeannie left so I wouldn't have to ask her. Shakespeare is saying that in the Seventh Age a person is *without everything*. When you're growing up, you've got a lot to look forward to, like being able to live any way you want without parents telling you what to do all the time, and like knowing practically everything, and like having a neat job and maybe being famous or something. And then you get old and start being like a baby again, but this time there isn't anything to look forward to. This time you look backwards and remember how you used to be, only you aren't like that anymore. It must be like being rich for a very long time and then being poor all of a sudden. It wouldn't be so bad if you didn't keep remembering how it was to be rich. Maybe that's why Grandpa has always made such a big deal about keeping his body in shape. Maybe he's been trying to avoid the Seventh Age.

It's all so depressing! It's hard to imagine being old when I don't even know how it feels to be just plain grown up, but looking at all these pictures of all these people who were living real lives every single day, just like me, but who are either dead or really old now, gives me a creepy feeling. I guess I never really thought about dying before. Not *me* dying, anyway, or Mom or Dad or Matt dying. Not even Grandpa dying—at least not really what it would be like. Now that's just about all I can think about. It's late, and I want to go to bed, but I don't want to, because sleeping seems too much like dying all of a sudden, and I'm too depressed. I think I will just sit up all night and try not to think about it!

FRIDAY, AUGUST 1, 2:00 p.m.

People are funny. Last night I was worrying about going to sleep and zap, all of a sudden it was morning. Some things you can't do anything about!

A couple of weeks ago this summer was just like any other summer, nothing much happening except I'd decided to be a butterfly champion. Now there are so many changes and so much to think about that every day seems to be important some way or other.

This morning Jeannie and I went to the library to begin Project Sophie. And we found out about genealogy. We walked in the main door and Jeannie went right to the reference department. I'd never even been to the reference department, because even though I like to read, libraries make me nervous.

Anyway, Jeannie just went right up to the reference desk and told the lady she was working on a historical novel and needed some help with background material. Maybe Jeannie gives off genius vibrations or something because practically the minute she opens her mouth grown-ups start listening to her as if she's going to say something they've always wanted to know. It turned out this particular person was exactly the right person to ask because her favorite thing is "genealogy." She even teaches a course in it at night. Jeannie asked her what genealogy was. Now that's one of the things about her. She is the smartest kid I know, but when the lady said a word she didn't understand, she just asked her what it meant. I'd have nodded my head a lot and pretended I knew what it meant and looked it up sometime later. I guess that's how Jeannie gets to know so much. Later, when the woman said another word I didn't know I started to ask her what it meant, but Jeannie already seemed to know, and the question got stuck in my throat and I started nodding again. Now I don't even remember the word. I will never be a genius!

Genealogy is the study of family histories. The librarian says a lot of people are interested in it now. Some of them are looking for rich or famous ancestors or trying to find out if they have a family crest or something. But most people just want to know more about their families—just like we want to know more about Sophie.

"Why do you think so many people are interested in their families lately?" Jeannie asked.

And she couldn't have asked a better question if she wanted to get this lady started. Her eyes lit up and she told us all about how our society has moved away from what she called the "extended family."

"People don't have roots anymore, the way they used to," she said. "A company moves a man to another state, sometimes clear across the continent, and families get split up. Older people don't live with their children and grandchildren the way they used to. And when they visit, no one has time for storytelling. Television has changed things, too. It used to be that there was nothing to do between supper and bedtime except talk or play games. And the older people told stories about when they were children."

By the time she'd finished talking about the extended family, I had the feeling that having Grandpa live with us made us the luckiest people in town, except that we had mostly wasted our luck because we'd been too busy watching TV to listen to his stories. I didn't tell her about homework and swimming and baseball and Matt's place in the basement and Dad and his newspaper and Mom's job. Even if we'd never had the TV set on in our lives, I don't think there would have been all that much time to listen to Grandpa. And I'm not sure he'd have wanted to tell stories anyway. But she thought she had it all figured out, so I didn't want to act like I doubted her.

"When people began to realize how little they knew about their families, they began to want to know more. I think it's a real human need to have roots—to know where you came from and what life was like for the people who lived before you."

She told us about going to city hall and getting records. And looking for church records of baptisms and funerals and stuff. And she even said that sometimes you can learn a whole lot from visiting cemeteries. She also showed us where in the library to get general stuff about the times—what kinds of houses they had, what things had been invented then and what hadn't. By the time we left the library, Jeannie was starting to wonder about her own family. I could tell that Project Sophie wasn't nearly so important to her as it had been. All that about city hall and visiting cemeteries turned me off. It sounded much duller than looking at Grandpa's albums. But that librarian had worked on Jeannie as if she had the flu—after being around her Jeannie had caught it, too.

Last year in school I read a book where a twelve-year-old girl went back in time more than a hundred years. She walked out into a vacant lot and when she came to the sidewalk on the other side it was a hundred years earlier. Now that was exciting! A lot more fun than poking around in some city records looking for death certificates and stuff. That's what I want to do with Sophie. I want to walk into a picture and be with her—as long as I can be sure I can get back when I want to.

Anyhow, when Jeannie went home for lunch she was talking about going to city hall this afternoon. She didn't say so, but I guess she's going to do her own family history. I said I didn't feel like going. I was feeling kind of bad that she wouldn't be telling Sophie's story, because I know I'll never be able to do it. I don't write worth a darn. But I know for sure this genealogy stuff is exactly the kind of thing Jeannie likes to do best, so I can't really blame her. She isn't all that hot about swimming, but she's never bugged me about how much time I spend at the pool. And lots of times she goes with me and writes in her journal while I swim. I guess you can't share everything, not even with your very best friend!

When I got home, Mom said that Dad wants

us to have a family meeting after supper. We've never had one before. It's supposed to be a good way to handle all the problems families have, and meetings like that are supposed to be democratic, with kids having an equal vote. But I can't imagine it working with us. Mostly Mom and Dad make the decisions and Matt and I have to live with them whether we like it or not. Actually, except for not getting to go on vacations, I can't think of anything they've decided that I don't go along with. And they mostly know how we feel about everything anyway. At least they used to, before Matt decided to shut himself off from everybody.

Maybe this is Dad's way to get Matt more involved. I'll bet it doesn't work, though. I sure hope I don't get like Matt when I get to be his age.

The meeting is going to be about Grandpa, and whether it gets Matt involved or not, I'm not much looking forward to it.

FRIDAY, AUGUST 1, 11:00 p.m.

Well, the meeting is over. And if Dad wanted Matt to get more involved, it worked. But I can't say that things are much better than they were before. And it wasn't the kind of thing I'd want to go through again.

Mom had arranged for Grandpa to go to Mr. Buhler's for the evening, so we wouldn't have to worry about him hearing us. Dad started out by telling us everything Grandpa's doctor has told them. It's like Shakespeare said. Grandpa's starting to be in his second childhood. But it's partly what I thought at first, too. It's partly that he's crazy. At least it's called *senile dementia,* and "dementia" means craziness. "Senile" is being old. The doctor says it doesn't happen to everybody—in fact, it doesn't happen to very many people, really. No one is quite sure why it happens to some people, but they're doing a lot of research about it to see if they can keep it from happening or give somebody medicine or do an operation to stop it after it has started happening. Some people think it happens because the brain is just sort of drying up, and other people think it has to do with arteries getting clogged up so oxygen can't get to the brain the way it should, and other people have found other kinds of physical things that can cause it. Some of those can be cured and some can't. Anyway, right now most people who get that way are put into nursing homes because they can't live alone and not many families are able to take care of them. Sometimes people have to be strapped into their beds at night to keep them from getting up and ruining things or hurting themselves.

When Dad said that, I looked at Mom and her eyes were shiny—like she was going to cry, but she didn't. Then, before Dad had a chance to go on, Matt jumped right up out of his chair and yelled, "You can't do that to Grandpa! You can't tie him up like some kind of animal! *He* wouldn't do that to anybody! He wouldn't even do that to a dog!" I sat very still and watched Matt. He was actually crying. And I began to wonder if I'd been wrong about him all along. I thought he hadn't noticed anything wrong with Grandpa, or at least didn't care. But maybe shutting himself away was his way of keeping everybody from knowing how much he cared.

I thought Dad would yell but he didn't do anything at first. Then he got up and went over to Matt and put his arms around him just like he was a little kid and hugged him. Matt started crying even harder and hugged Dad back. It was Mom who went on.

"Matt, nobody wants to do that to Grandpa. That's why he's lived with us all these years. We never wanted him to go to a nursing home. And nobody wants to have to decide what we have to decide, either. But we have a problem, and we have to find some way to solve it."

Dad gave Matt his handkerchief and sat him back down in his chair. Then he started talking again. "You and Kerry both know that I've always been more willing than your mother to consider a nursing home. But since Grandpa is your mother's father, I didn't think I had a right to push. But now . . ."

"He's not crazy!" Matt interrupted in this very low voice that sounded angry and sad at the same time.

Mom answered him. "Not really, Matt. But he has been doing some crazy things. And he will do them again."

"Maybe he'll get better," Matt said.

"No." Mom's eyes were shiny again. "He will get worse. There will come a time when he won't even know who we are."

"And before that there will be crazier and crazier things," Dad said. "He's fallen into the pool already. He might walk out in front of a car. You saw the mess he made the other morning . . ."

Matt started to interrupt again, but Dad rushed on. "And we know you did the same thing when you were little. But you were growing every day, and every day getting less and less likely to make that kind of mess again. Grandpa is going the other way. Every day he will get more and more likely to make that kind of mess. And worse ones. We would not be able to trust him alone in the house, day or night."

"We could get babysitters!" Matt said. But he didn't sound like he believed that even when he said it.

"We need to explain things a little better, I think," Mom said. "Grandpa has had a long life, and most of that life has been happy and productive. He had to overcome a lot of hardships when he was young. It would be wonderful if he could live out the rest of his life happily, with his family around him. He deserves that. Everybody does. But his brain is not letting things happen that way. Many people die before they are as old as he is, and they don't have to live through what is happening to him. Many other people just never encounter this. If life were fair, he wouldn't either. But Grandpa is becoming like a child again . . ."

"The Seventh Age," I said before I could stop myself. I didn't want to do anything but listen at this meeting, but it just popped out.

Dad looked surprised. "Kerry has been reading Shakespeare," he said. And then he quoted the last bit of the speech. ". . . sans everything," he finished, and then repeated it. "Sans everything."

"You have no idea what that will mean, Matt," Mom went on. "You've never had to care for a baby. But from now on, Grandpa will become more and more like a baby, and require more and more of the kind of care a baby needs." She paused. "There will almost certainly come a time when he'll have to be put in diapers."

Matt turned around in his chair and pushed his face against the upholstery.

"There would have to be someone to stay up with him every night to be sure he didn't get out of bed. And someone would have to be at home with him all day or go with him if he went to the park."

"I could," Matt muttered into the chair.

"School will start soon," Dad reminded him.

"And your father and I both have to work," Mom added.

I'd been thinking about what the librarian had said about the way things had changed for families since the time of the extended family, and I could see that Mom and Dad weren't getting through to Matt. "Listen, Matt," I said, and then wondered what I could say next. But somehow, when I opened my mouth words just came out without me even knowing for sure what they were going to be. "You want Grandpa to stay here and things to be the way they used to be. So do I. We love him. But maybe you aren't thinking about the way things have really been around here lately. Maybe you're remembering how things were when we were little and spent so much time with him. Now we have school and our friends, and you have baseball. How would we have time to take care of him when we haven't even had the time to go rock hunting with him? The librarian told us today that a long time ago families all lived together, and there were always lots of aunts and uncles and cousins around, so when somebody got sick or old there were plenty of people around to take care of him. Like there were plenty of people to take care of the children. But hardly anybody lives that way anymore. It isn't our fault, it isn't Grandpa's fault, it's just the way things have changed. We're luckier than most kids—at least we know Grandpa. But we sure haven't done much for him lately."

Then I guessed I'd said the wrong thing, because even with his back turned, I could tell Matt was crying again. It made my stomach all twisted to see Matt crying, because he honestly believes that boys don't cry, and he hasn't cried, or let anybody see him cry, since he was about six.

"It isn't your fault, Matt. Or mine. We have to grow up and have our own friends and our own lives. Grandpa had to grow up and away from Sophie, too. He understands."

All of a sudden, I thought I understood something about Sophie and Grandpa. I was beginning to see why he had never told us about her.

Matt turned and looked at Mom then, and his face had a kind of squeezed look. "I don't see why you had this meeting at all! It's going to be just like always. You and Dad have decided what to do already and it doesn't matter what I think. You don't even want to know how I feel!"

I wasn't watching Matt by this time, because just as he started talking Dad stood up again, and this time he was really mad.

"Suppose you let us finish before you tell us what we have decided, Matthew. You seem to want to keep this 'family' together all of a sudden, but you're really thinking of no one but yourself. And you forget that this man we all love is not your own private property. He is not just your grandfather. He is your mother's father. Do us the justice to believe that we are seriously concerned for his welfare and not looking for an easy way out for ourselves."

I noticed that Dad's hands were shaking, but I couldn't tell if that was because he was so angry or for some other reason. One thing I did know—I was glad he wasn't talking to me. And even though I knew Dad was right, I was sorry for Matt.

Mother was talking again, and Dad began pacing. "Dr. Harris says that Grandpa is in incredibly good health otherwise. All these years of taking care of himself have given him a body that is nowhere near wearing out. It could be years before Grandpa's body is as old as his brain. It wouldn't mean looking after him for a few months—it could mean as long as the rest of your high school years and till after you've gone away to college. Maybe even longer. Some families manage, Dr. Harris says, but most can't. And sometimes those families end up resenting the person they once loved enough to keep with them. It's something to think about. How much would you—could you give up?" Then she looked at me, and for a minute it was like she had been reading my mind. "And you, Kerry? How would you feel about people seeing you taking your grandfather back and forth to the park? How would you feel at the pool?"

Matt was still scowling. "I told you. You've already decided to send him away. What do you want from me? A pat on the back?"

I could hardly believe what he was saying. Hadn't he heard anything anybody had said? Dad was standing at the window and didn't seem to be paying attention this time. So Mom answered. "No. We have *not* decided anything. We still have some time. It could be several months before things get beyond what we can handle ourselves, without changing anything major. But whatever we decide, we must do it together, because no matter how much families may have changed, we *are* a family, and each of us will have to bear the burden of the decision. Eventually, of course, the decision must be made. We can keep him home and try to manage—I'd have to quit work and you would probably have to give up your extra activities at school. Or we could hire someone to live here and help us do what we can't do ourselves. Or we could find the best possible home for him."

For once, Matt didn't say anything. I wanted to keep quiet too, but I had a question I just had to ask, no matter what anybody thought. "Grandpa's not here tonight. Does he know what we're talking about? Does he know what's happening to him? Does *he* have a choice?"

For the second time, I'd said the wrong thing. Now Mom was crying. But it was too late to take it back, and besides, I wanted to know!

Dad turned back from the window. "That may be the hardest question we have to answer," he said. "He's an adult; he certainly should have the right to choose. But that choice may be too hard for him. It wouldn't be fair to make him choose between what he wants and what he thinks would be best for us. He may not be absolutely sure what is happening, but he certainly knows something is wrong. And he must suspect what kind of a burden he will become eventually. A baby can't feel guilty about the work his mother has to do to take care of him. But Grandpa would. And he has lived all his life with the fact that he became a burden to Sophie when she was only twelve, at a time when he didn't even know enough to be grateful. Do you think he would want to do that again?"

Matt got up and left the room then. A minute later, we heard the basement door slam. Dad sighed, and I wondered whether he was more worried about Grandpa or about Matt. I wanted to hug Mom and say something to her, but I didn't know what to say, so I just came on up to my room, thinking that I'd been wrong about growing up all this time. You don't know all the right answers at all. I know now that no matter what Matt and I say, and no matter how much they want to let us help decide, they are the ones who *have* to choose. And of all their choices, there isn't a single one that isn't rotten.

SATURDAY, AUGUST 2, 9:00 a.m.

Last night I had a dream. Most people wouldn't think that's very surprising, but for me it is, because I can hardly ever remember dreaming. Sometimes, when I first sit up in bed, I have a feeling that I could remember something if I think hard enough, but the minute I try, even that feeling goes away. It's like riding in a car on a hot day. Way up ahead the road looks wet and wavy, but if you watch it, the wet look disappears as you get closer.

But this morning when I woke up the whole dream was still there like a book I had just read and could remember page by page. I was swimming the butterfly stroke at the pool—in some kind of big, important meet. Lots of people were standing around the pool cheering for me, but I couldn't take the time to look and see who they were, or I'd slow down and lose the race. So I just kept swimming and hearing the noise until I reached to touch the wall of the pool to turn around. Then I looked up and saw Sophie standing there. She was holding a big kettle of something steamy, like soup, in one hand, and with the other she was holding a little boy's arm to keep him from falling into the pool. At first I thought she was trying to keep Grandpa from falling in again, but I looked at the boy's face and it wasn't Grandpa at all, it was Matt. She said, "Come now, it's time for supper," and I just walked out of the water, because the pool had turned into a lake and I was following them up this sandy beach. When I got to where Sophie was putting the kettle over a campfire, I started to ask her where Grandpa was, but when she turned around, it wasn't Sophie at all anymore. It was Mom. Matt was sitting next to the fire, crying and crying, and Mom told me to take care of him because Sophie had gone home to help her mother. I kept trying to ask where Grandpa was, but all Matt would do was cry, and Mom was stirring the soup and wouldn't talk. So I took Matt's hand and we started to walk down the beach and he stopped crying and said he wanted Grandpa. He was still littler than me, and I was feeling that I had to take special care of him. But when I went to put my arm around him, he grew up all of a sudden and pushed me away. Then he ran off down the beach, and when I started to go after him, the beach turned into the park and a lot of kids who swim at the pool, including Kevin, were standing around laughing at me. I tried to ask where Matt was, but then I couldn't remember whether I was looking for Matt or Grandpa, and they went right on laughing. That was when I woke up.

Jeannie remembers a lot of her dreams and is always trying to analyze them and decide what they mean. So I tried to analyze this one, and I've worked and worked and can't figure it out. I quess it shows how surprised I was that Matt cried last night. But I can't figure out why people kept changing into other people or why we were having soup on a beach. Maybe it had something to do with the fact that Sophie could cook and I can't. Maybe part of why Matt was little was because I've been trying to imagine what it would be like to be Sophie and have to take care of a little brother who was scared and unhappy. Anyway, the main thing the dream proved to me is that I'm all mixed up.

Since I first heard about Sophie, I've thought I would have to work very hard to understand her and suddenly, last night, I found out that I don't even understand my brother. If you can't know a person you live with every single day, how could you know a person who's been dead for years and years? Anyway, now that I know Matt does care, I've decided I ought to talk to him about Grandpa.

SATURDAY, AUGUST 2, 9:30 p.m.

I think the reason people do genealogy is because they can figure out the people who lived a long time ago better than they can figure out the people who are living with them. I tried to talk to Matt after he came home from the park tonight. He at least let me into his basement room! But then he wouldn't talk about Grandpa at all. Maybe he was embarrassed that I'd seen him cry, but it's no wonder I didn't know before how he feels about Grandpa. If someone had been listening to us, they'd have thought he didn't care at all. He said he didn't want to talk about it and that it wasn't our problem anyhow, no matter what Mom and Dad said. I asked him if he had ever wondered what Grandpa was like when he was a kid, or what the family was like then. I thought I'd connected. He looked as if he might want to know. But then he seemed to remember that he wasn't interested in anything, and he put his earphones on. After that there wasn't any point in staying down there with him, since he couldn't hear anything I said anyway.

Our third grade teacher used to say that you have to walk a mile in somebody's shoes before you can know why they act the way they do. But I can't see any way to get into Matt's shoes in the first place. He won't even let me see them! The only thing I can figure is that he wants to stay out of it so he won't have to take any of the blame for whatever is finally decided. Anyway, I've given up on him.

Jeannie came over for lunch and we took sandwiches to the park. I still haven't gone to the pool, but I can't very well stay away from the whole park for my whole life. I told her my dream and she was really interested, but her ideas weren't any better than mine for a change. She has started on her family history, and apologized for running out on me with Sophie, but I told her it was okay. It happened to me first, so I guess I ought to be able to understand how it is to get interested in your own family. Her mother found her a lot of photographs and even some letters. And she's going to write to Jeannie's grandparents and some of the aunts and uncles, because she thinks there may be some diaries around. Talk about luck! I guess Sophie didn't have much time to keep a diary. Things like that must run in Jeannie's family. The lady at the library told her she should get a tape recorder and go around to all her relatives and get them to tell her everything they can remember. Her mother is going to lend her the money to get a cassette recorder right away. She's really turned on about the whole thing. Maybe she can get extra credit for it at school this year, too.

She went back to the library this afternoon, but I didn't feel like going along. I'm not very interested in historical background anymore. What I want to know about is how everybody felt about everybody else. Dad says that Grandpa feels guilty about Sophie. And that's why I think he hasn't talked about her much. But I wonder how she felt about him—and the others. I wonder if she hated to quit being a kid and start acting like a mother to the other kids. I wonder if she loved them and wanted so much to keep the family together that she didn't mind all the work. And I wonder how she felt when they all grew up and left her alone. She wouldn't have had time to make a life of her own until they were grown. They all got married. But she never did.

I wonder what she wanted to be when she grew up. I'll bet after all that mothering she had to do she wouldn't have wanted to be a wife and mother anyway. Or maybe that's all she ever wanted to be. She sure must have known how to be one! I guess there weren't many women working back then. Or if they did work it was like in that factory, not like the way it is with Mom, doing what she wants to do. And I wonder when Sophie looked back on her life if she was glad it had been the way it was.

My brain is tired. I went to the library after supper and got three science fiction books. I'm going to quit thinking about Sophie and Grandpa and Matt and Mom and Dad and everybody! I'm just going to read.

MONDAY, AUGUST 4, 9:30 p.m.

The most incredible thing happened tonight! I was in my room reading when Matt walked in. Matt! In my room! And nobody had sent him up or anything.

"You got a minute?" he asked, like he would go back downstairs in ten seconds if I said no and be just as happy.

So I told him I had a minute and put away my book. He came and sat on my bed.

"It's about Grandpa," he said, as if I hadn't guessed that much. "I don't think any of the choices Mom and Dad said we had are any good."

I just nodded.

"Because we have to let him choose what he's going to do, don't we?"

I didn't know what to say, because that's the way I'd been feeling, but I thought I could see why Dad didn't think it would be fair.

"I mean, he's a grown man. And I don't care about this 'second childhood' thing. He isn't a child! Oh, I know he's been doing crazy things. There are some that Mom and Dad don't even know about . . ."

"Have you seen—?" I asked, and he just nodded.

"I've been watching him for a long time now, and I can tell when he's about to do something crazy. There's something different in his eyes. I can't explain it, exactly, but I can see it. But when he's his old self, he's still as sharp as ever. He's run his own life all these years. We have no right to start running it for him! I've talked to him about it."

"Matt, when?" I couldn't believe it. I hadn't even thought about talking directly to Grandpa.

"Yesterday. And today some. Oh, not exactly about what's been happening to him, but what it's like to get old. I went for a couple of walks with him and we talked about it. He says that when you get old, you kind of lose track of yourself. Kerry, he understands all about it. It happened to his father."

This was something I didn't know about. Mom had never mentioned it, and I wondered if she knew.

"His father wasn't all that old when it happened to him, but Grandpa says it happens to different people at different times. And some people who have had a rough time in life lose themselves sooner than other people. He says his father never really recovered after his mother died. He lived a pretty long time, and he went to work every day, and he came home at night and to everybody outside the family he seemed okay. But the kids knew he had changed. He didn't pay much attention to any of them—just let Sophie do everything. He kept on supporting them until Grandpa finally got old enough to leave home and take a job, and then he just quit. He stayed home all the time."

"But where'd the money come from then?" I asked, imagining how it would be for Sophie to have all the kids grown up and out of the house finally and then to have to start worrying about money.

"By that time the others all had jobs or were married and everybody chipped in as much money as they could to take care of Sophie and their father. Grandpa doesn't talk about Sophie much, I know, but he talked about her a little. She took care of the house and her father and took in washing besides. It got harder and harder for her because he began to do crazy things. The other kids tried to help, and they all lived close, but he was pretty hard to manage, and Sophie was the one who was living right in the house with him. Anyway, before he got completely crazy, he got sick. He was in bed all the time, and partly it was easier for Sophie to handle him, but partly it was harder, because he couldn't do anything for himself at all, and she had to nurse him all the time. Finally he died. And so did Sophie."

This was news to me. I knew Sophie died a long time ago, but I didn't know anything about how it happened.

"Did she get sick too? What happened?"

"Grandpa says she didn't get sick—at least not like their father. By that time everybody was married and Grandpa's other sister had moved to Wisconsin with her family. Grandpa and Grandma had their three kids and Grandpa wasn't able to give Sophie as much money as he had before. Grandpa said it was like she had done everything she had to do. She had raised the kids and cared for their father, and they had all left her, so there wasn't anything left for her to do except die."

"That's impossible. People just don't die like that!"

"Well, anyway, that's what Grandpa said, and I couldn't get him to say another thing about

Sophie. But don't you see, he knows about what's happening to him, because it happened to his own father. And he knows about how families take care of the person it happens to. We've got to let him know we care and we trust him to decide what he wants."

I guess I nodded because Matt got up from the bed and said that we'd have to talk to Mom and Dad, and then he was gone. I wasn't paying much attention, though, because I was trying to put together what Matt had told me and what Dad had said about Grandpa feeling guilty about Sophie. If I'd been thinking about what Matt said, I'd never have nodded, because I understood then what Dad had said about the choice being unfair to Grandpa. He knew better than anyone how hard it is for a family to have to take care of somebody like that when they have their own lives to lead. Grandpa wouldn't want anyone ever to have to do that again—especially not for him. More than ever, I could see that there wasn't a single right choice to make, but the worst one of all would be to make Grandpa decide.

TUESDAY, AUGUST 5, 9:00 a.m.

This morning Grandpa came into my room with the photo albums and a little velvet box. The minute he came in, I looked to see if there was anything funny about the way he was dressed. But he was in ordinary clothes. I hadn't gotten up yet, so he sat down on my bed.

For a while, he just sat there, holding the albums and the box and staring out the window. Then he seemed to remember what he came in for. "Sophie," he said, "I've brought back your things." I looked at him again, but there was nothing strange about the way he was dressed, and I couldn't see anything different in his eyes. And his voice was normal. But he was calling me

Sophie. I couldn't understand it. I just smiled at him.

He put the albums down on the bed. "These are Father's, and I thought you'd want them back now. We have to keep the family things together. And Sophie, you mustn't feel so bad about Father dying. It takes a person an entire lifetime to find out who he is. It's terrible to lose that, like he did. He wasn't himself anymore, Sophie. It's all right. The person he really was died a long time ago."

I didn't know what I could say, so I just nodded. He sat for a minute, rubbing the velvet box with one hand. Then he picked it up and handed it to me. "And here's your locket. I can't think how I came to have it with my things, but you'd better have it back. I wouldn't want anything to happen to it. You take it and keep it always. It belongs to you!"

I started to tell him to keep it, that I was Kerry, not Sophie. But something in the way he was looking at me made me stop. I swear he wasn't being crazy just then. He was Grandpa, and he was doing something he wanted to do. He didn't really think I was Sophie at all. But why was he pretending? I took the box from him, but didn't open it. Then he learned over and kissed me on the cheek. "Good-bye, Sophie," he said. "Take good care of your locket—always."

Then he got up and went out. I stared at the door for a minute after he left, trying to figure out what that had been all about, but it didn't make sense, so I opened the box. Inside was a golden locket with a cameo. All of a sudden I remembered it. Sophie had been wearing it in Grandpa's christening picture. I opened it, and there were two pictures inside—one of Sophie's mother, looking even younger and softer than in the album, and the other of her father, also young, with a handlebar mustache. On the back was an inscription—"To our oldest child, our treasure forever."

I ran downstairs to tell Mom and Dad, but they weren't up yet. I didn't see Grandpa anywhere, so I went to Matt's room and knocked on his door, very quietly, in case he was still asleep. The moment I knocked, he opened the door, like he had been just about to come out anyway. He was still in his pajamas too, and was holding Grandpa's gold pocketwatch and chain.

"What's that?" I asked, but he just grabbed my arm and pulled me into his room and shut the door.

"Grandpa was here," he said. "He was talking like he was crazy, but he wasn't."

I nodded. "I know. He came to my room, too!"

Matt held out the watch. "He called me Jonathan, and he gave me this."

“He called me Sophie and gave me her locket.”

“When?”

“Just a couple of minutes ago. I looked at the locket for a while and then went to the kitchen to tell Mom. I didn’t realize it was so early.”

“He must have come to my room just after. Didn’t you see him downstairs?”

“No. Maybe he’s in his room.”

Just then, we heard the back door. You can’t see the backyard from Matt’s room, so we ran back to mine and got to the window just in time to see Grandpa go out the gate in the direction of the park.

“Should we go after him?” I asked.

“I don’t think so,” Matt said. “I don’t care how he was talking, he didn’t look crazy. He knew exactly what he was doing.”

“That’s what I thought. I wonder why he was acting like that.”

“I don’t know, but I’m sure we don’t have to worry about him doing anything crazy at the park.”

We woke Mom and Dad then, and Mom thought we should go after him anyway, but Dad said that if Matt and I thought he was okay, we’d better let him go. Finally Mom agreed. She said it was bad enough for him to have us come after him when we had to, we’d better not follow him around when he was all right. I asked her what to do with the locket and the watch and the albums, and she said just to keep them. The pocketwatch isn't working anymore, and there isn't any reason he'd need the other things anyway.

So we all went down to the kitchen and had breakfast. But I didn't feel much like eating. I just can't get over the feeling that something is wrong. More wrong than ever. And I can tell by the way Matt picked at his breakfast that he feels the same way I do.

TUESDAY, AUGUST 5, 4:00 p.m.

Grandpa made his own choice.

Matt and I stuck around the house, not sure whether we should stay and wait for Grandpa to come home or go to the park and find him. Dad went to work and Mom stayed home. She said we could go to the park, but we shouldn't act as if we'd been sent to get him. We decided to wait till nearly lunchtime and say we had come to get him for lunch. Then we decided instead to take along a picnic and eat in the park. Matt went down to his basement room, but didn't play his stereo. David came over and went down, but came back up again and went away. Jeannie stopped by on her way to city hall, to see if I'd go with her, but of course, I didn't. Something was really bugging me, but I couldn't decide what it was. Finally, at around ten, I couldn't stand it any longer. I started to go down to see Matt, but he was on his way up.

"Let's go," he said. "I think something's wrong."

I just nodded and went with him. We were just going out the door when the phone rang.

I don't know how to explain it, but there was something about that ring. Matt noticed it, too. We stopped, and Mom answered it after that one ring. She said, "Hello," and then nothing. And then still nothing. But her face went white and kind of stiff. Finally, she swallowed, hard. "When?" she asked. Then she nodded a couple of times and closed her eyes. She listened for another minute or so and then hung up without saying another word. We just waited for what she was going to say, but we both knew what it was.

"Your grandfather is dead."

Even though I had known what she was going to say, when she said it, it was as if I couldn't understand the words. Matt nodded.

"They found him in the pool when they went to open it. They called the rescue squad immediately and gave him mouth-to-mouth resuscitation. The rescue squad gave him oxygen and did everything they could, but he was gone." Mom sat down on the chair by the phone. "I should have sent you after him this morning. You said he was talking crazy!"

"No!" Matt and I had both spoken at once. Matt went and put his hand on her shoulder. "He wasn't crazy when he left. Honest! We couldn't have known."

"There wasn't anything we could have done," I said, and I knew somehow that I was right. Even if we had gone after him this time, even if we had managed to bring him home.

"I just can't understand it," Mom said. "They said the pool gate was still locked."

For some reason, that made me cry, and then we were all crying. Finally, Mom said she would call Dad so they could make the arrangements. She was on the phone when I left the kitchen, and Matt was still with her. I went down to Grandpa's room and went in.

I didn't know why I wanted to go to his room, maybe just to feel closer to him or something. But once I went in, I knew I'd been right about what I'd been thinking. He had made his bed before he left. His closet door was open and his clothes were still hanging there, but everything from the closet shelves had been taken down and arranged around the room. His rock collection, neatly packed in its wooden box, stood on his desk. I opened the big center desk drawer and there were only pencils and paper clips and rubber bands and stuff. All the papers and letters and things he used to keep there were gone. All the boxes from the closet were labeled, most of them with names. There was one for Mom, one for Dad, one for Aunt Joan, one for Uncle Dan. There was even one labeled "discard." Nobody would have to sort through his things. He had done that himself. He must have stayed up all last night to do it.

I started to wonder if he had been sad, looking at all the things he had kept, and then I started to cry all over again. I guess I fell asleep on his bed, because it was much later when Dad came in. He looked around the room and nodded, but he didn't say anything. He went back out, and I came up to my room to look at Sophie's locket.

SATURDAY, AUGUST 9, 9:00 p.m.

Grandpa's funeral was yesterday. Everybody came, and everybody has gone home now. Nobody said much about what really happened at the pool, or even mentioned how neat everything was in his room—as though if we don't say anything out loud, we won't really know. Mom says I can keep the locket and Matt can keep the watch. That's how I know she knows. If he had really been crazy when he gave them to us, I don't think she would have let us keep them.

I've thought and thought about what Grandpa chose, and I'm not sure how I feel about it. I know there are lots of people who would say he chose wrong. It sure wasn't a choice that makes any of *us* feel good. It's more than just missing him, more than how empty the house feels. Sometimes I feel like maybe we could have done something different somehow and he might not have done what he did. And then I cry again. But maybe how bad we feel isn't really what's important. Maybe it's only important that Grandpa made his own choice.

I guess nobody can say what's right for anybody else. When Dad told Matt Grandpa wasn't Matt's property, he was only partly right. Grandpa wasn't anybody's property except his own. I keep remembering what he said that morning—about his father not being himself anymore when he died, and I know he was trying to explain things to me.

I also know that with Grandpa Shakespeare wasn't right after all. Grandpa wasn't "sans everything." He still had himself. He didn't let anybody take over his life. He didn't do what he did to keep from being a burden. He did it so he would never lose himself. My grandfather *wasn't* crazy!

Jeannie asked me if I wanted her to help me work on Project Sophie. She said she could always do her own family afterwards. But I don't think I want to do it anymore.

Matt was really different all during the funeral preparations. He helped Mom and Aunt

Joan, and talked to people who came to the funeral home and everything. But today he was back in his basement room with the stereo blaring. He didn't even use his earphones. David was over for a while, and Matt's going to play in a ball game next week. I guess he'll keep his feelings about Grandpa as much to himself as ever.

Sophie's locket is on my dresser. I put its box right between my lamp and the first swimming trophy I ever won. Maybe when I'm older I'll wear it, but I'm afraid I'd lose it now.

I went to the pool today, and Kevin is going to be my coach. I'll have to work hard to be ready for the meet, now that I've missed so many days. I kept thinking I'd look up from the pool and see Grandpa watching me, and then I'd remember and feel all hollow inside. I guess that'll happen for a while, until I'm used to the fact that he's dead.

I don't know much more now than I did before, but one thing I do know. A person has to live his own life and make his own decisions. I haven't decided what I want to do with my whole life yet, but right now what I most want to do is swim. And I'm going to win the butterfly event at that swimming meet. Maybe someday I'll win an Olympic Gold Medal, and maybe I won't. But either way, I'll be doing what I want to do, and I think Grandpa would be glad.